Welcome to Harlequin's great new series,
created by some of our bestselling authors
from Down Under:

THE AUSTRALIANS

Twelve tales of heated romance and adventure—
guaranteed to turn your whole world upside down!

Travel to an Outback cattle station, experience the
glamour of the Gold Coast or visit the bright lights
of Sydney where you'll meet twelve engaging young
women, all feisty and all about to face their biggest
challenge yet...falling in love.

And it will take some very special women to tame
our heroes! Strong, rugged, often infuriating and
always irresistible, they're one hundred percent prime
Australian male: hard to get close to...but even
harder to forget!

The Wonder from Down Under:
where spirited women win the hearts of
Australia's most independent men.

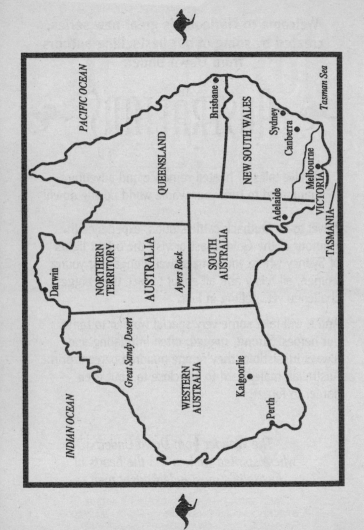

THE AUSTRALIANS

MALE FOR CHRISTMAS

Lynsey Stevens

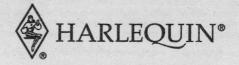

HARLEQUIN®

TORONTO • NEW YORK • LONDON
AMSTERDAM • PARIS • SYDNEY • HAMBURG
STOCKHOLM • ATHENS • TOKYO • MILAN • MADRID
PRAGUE • WARSAW • BUDAPEST • AUCKLAND

ISBN 0-373-82578-1

MALE FOR CHRISTMAS

First North American Publication 1998.

Printed in U.S.A.

Lynsey Stevens was born in Brisbane, Queensland, and before beginning to write she was a librarian. It was in secondary school that she decided she wanted to be a writer. "Writers, I imagined," Lynsey explains, "lived such exciting lives: traveling to exotic places, making lots of money and not having to work. I have traveled. However, the taxman loves me dearly and no one told me about typist's backache and frustrating lost words!" When she's not writing she enjoys reading and cross-stitching and she's interested in genealogy.

PROLOGUE

TAYLA sat in her study working on her next article. She gazed absently at the computer screen as she tried to keep her attention focused.

It was almost Christmas. And for some reason this thought made her feel sad. Although why it did she didn't know. Christmas was a fun-filled family occasion of eating traditional goodies, opening presents, of Christmas carols and watching cricket while trying to get cool in the relentless Australian summer. It wasn't a time to feel unhappy.

Maybe she was a little melancholy because they were breaking with family tradition this year. Usually they all went up to the mountain to Nan's and the huge old family home but this year Nan was coming down to Tayla in Brisbane.

Tayla would have those she loved most around her. Her daughter, her niece and Nan. Only the venue had changed and Christmas was still Christmas, she told herself. So what was wrong with her?

Since Mike's death Tayla had actually begun to enjoy family Christmases again. Her late husband had not been family or tradition oriented so Christmas during her married life had taken on a seemingly incongruous tension. Somewhat guiltily Tayla realised she had relaxed again, felt the wonder of being with her family at this special time.

So there was no need to be depressed, was there? And yet— Perhaps lately she had been beginning to feel just a little lonely....

CHAPTER ONE

'THIS *is* just going to be for the weekend, isn't it?'

Tayla Greer shot a quick glance at her daughter before returning her attention to the highway. 'That's the plan.'

Carey groaned. 'And that could mean yes or no or a possible maybe.'

'I thought you liked visiting Nan,' Tayla put in. 'And it is her eighty-eighth birthday.'

'I know. And I do like being with Nan. She's great. It's the rest of this clan that bore me witless.'

'Most of the rest of the family won't be there.'

'Promises. Promises,' Carey muttered.

'Your uncle Adrian and aunt Simone have taken young Charlie down to visit his grandparents in Tassie.'

'You know, Uncle Adrian even brasses Nan off, Mum.'

Tayla couldn't deny her brother did tend toward pompousness but she knew she should make a token effort to curb her daughter's relentless honesty. However, in the interests of peace she decided to let that one pass. 'There'll only be you and I and your cousin, Rachel.'

Carey gave an exclamation of disgust. 'What if Aunt Marlene comes home?'

'Rachel's mother is in Italy. You know that.'

'And you know we can't trust her. She's very unreliable. No one would ever guess you two were sisters, that's for sure.'

'Well, I assure you we are.' Tayla ran a hand through

8

her longish auburn hair, knowing her daughter spoke the truth. Tayla and her sister, Marlene, older by eight years, were totally unalike. Tayla was tall and, well, statuesque would be a kind description, she decided derisively. She took after her father's family, Nan said, while Marlene was small and fine-boned like their mother.

'I'm not staying if Aunt Marlene *does* come home,' Carey stated firmly.

'She's on her honeymoon in Venice. Could you see her cutting that short?'

Carey laughed. 'It is her fourth, Mum. She must be able to do honeymoons with her eyes closed. Gosh! Now there's an interesting thought. Adds new dimensions to the old saying, ''They're all the same in the dark,'' don't you think, Mum?'

'Carey, please.'

'At least this one's only four years younger than she is. Remember the last one? He was twenty years younger and that was all off in a year. Still.' Carey grinned lewdly and wiggled her eyebrows. 'It must have been fun for her while it lasted.'

'That's enough, Carey.' Tayla frowned at her daughter and the young girl sighed.

'Why do you think Aunt Marlene marries them, Mum? I mean, why go to all that trouble? Why doesn't she just sleep with them and then move on? It'd save all those legal hassles.'

'Now what's a mother of a sixteen-year-old daughter expected to say to that, hmm?' Tayla asked dryly and Carey's young face broke into a reluctant smile.

'Probably stuff involving promiscuous, unsafe, et cetera, et cetera. How's that?'

'It'll do for a start.' Tayla bit her lip. 'You could have asked Brett to come along with us this weekend if you'd wanted to. I would have spoken to his parents, told them you'd be supervised.'

Carey rolled her eyes. 'Oh, great, Mum. That would have done wonders for my image.'

'What image is that?'

'I don't want to talk about it.' Carey folded her arms. 'Maybe I just didn't want to ask Brett.'

'Oh. Is this the end of a beautiful romance?'

'Very funny, Mum. And pretty insensitive to my young adolescent feelings, too, if you believe all the books. How do you know I'm not broken-hearted?'

'After the lunch you put away? Not likely.' Tayla chuckled. 'Believe me, I checked for all signs of languishment.'

'Brett and I just decided to cool it for a while. No big deal. It's not as though we're engaged or anything.'

'I'm relieved to hear that. Sixteen is a little young to be making a lifetime commitment.'

'Get real, Mum.'

'I did like Brett though.'

'Then perhaps you should give him a call,' Carey put in succinctly. 'Maybe he's looking for an older woman to get a bit of experience.'

'Is that what this is all about? Did Brett put the hard word on you and—'

'The hard word? Oh, good grief!' Carey groaned.

'Sorry. Is your old mother dating herself? What do they call it these days?'

Carey muttered under her breath.

'Seriously, love. You know you don't have to let yourself be blackmailed into having sex if you don't want to. And if Brett's into that sort of emotional coercion he's not worth worrying about.'

'It's his age, Mum. He can't help his hormones.'

'What about yours? You know, Carey, growing up—'

'Mum! Please!' Carey held up her hand. 'Don't put yourself through this. It's no problem. I'm not having sex with Brett because I don't want to.'

Tayla breathed a silent sigh of relief.

'I told him I realised that sexually he was at his peak but unfortunately women aren't at my age. That's how it is. He has to live with it.'

'What about curiosity, as in yours?'

'I can control that.'

'I see. So I take it Brett's now looking for a woman who's reached her sexual crest, too. Hence your older women crack.'

'It's a known fact that women reach their peak in their thirties so—' Carey shrugged and turned her hazel eyes contemplatively on her mother. 'That means I should be worrying about you.'

'Me?' Tayla laughed spontaneously as she pulled out to pass a slower car.

'Well, you are thirty-four. The most dangerous time I'd have said.'

'I'm nearly thirty-five. And I'm quite happy without those sorts of complications, thank you very much.'

There was a moment of silence before Carey spoke again. 'Do you think you'll marry again, Mum?' she asked softly. 'I mean, it's been five years since Dad died and I'll be going to university in a year or two. Don't you think you might get lonely?'

'I don't have time to be lonely,' Tayla replied lightly.

'What about sex? Don't you miss it?'

'Carey!'

'Okay. Okay.' Carey shifted in her seat. 'But it seems a shame to waste your sexual peak. It's probably down-hill all the way from now on.'

'There's a blue Lancer. I thought it might have been Rachel.'

'New subject, Mum?'

'I think so, don't you?'

Carey exhaled with feeling. 'It wouldn't be Rachel's Lancer. She's not coming up to Nan's until tomorrow.'

'Since when?'

'She rang yesterday. I forgot to tell you.'

'Carey, I told you to write down any phone messages.'

'It's no big deal, Mum.'

'It could have been about one of my stories,' Tayla began.

'I would have told you that. Really, Mum.'

Tayla sighed and bit back the urge to nag her daughter. 'What did Rachel say?'

'Just that we'll have to wait until tomorrow to meet the new man, Mr. Wonderful. She said something had come up and that they wouldn't be there until tomorrow.'

'She's bringing this man she's been dating then?'

'Yes. His name's Mac something. She's been seeing him for a few months.'

'A few months?' Tayla shot a glance at her daughter. Her niece, Rachel, was almost like a daughter to Tayla and she always told Tayla everything. At least she had in the past. 'I haven't heard about him,' she said evenly.

'She only told me about him last week,' Carey remarked offhandedly. 'She said she wanted us to just meet him, not have any preconceived ideas about him, or some such rubbish. What does it matter what we think? She has to live with him.'

'Live with him? Is it that serious?'

'It was a figure of speech, Mum. She hasn't even slept with him.'

'Slept with him?' Tayla felt she was losing her hold on the conversation, something she felt quite often these days when talking to her daughter.

'Mum, you're a worrywart.' Carey sighed exaggerat-edly. 'You know Rachel is rebelling against her mother's promiscuity by being almost nunlike,' she stated with arrogant youthful conviction. 'Sounds like cutting off your nose to spite your face, if you ask me. Anyway, Rachel says she's in love. Yuck!' Carey exclaimed de-risively. 'And I have a feeling she's going to be mooning around looking all dreamy so if she wants to talk about bridesmaids and frilly dresses, then—'

'Rachel said she wants to marry this man?' Tayla broke in.

'Well.' Carey hesitated. 'She didn't exactly say that. I was just saying that'll probably be the next thing.'

'And I think you're getting a little ahead of yourself. Rachel hasn't known this man long enough to be think-ing of marriage.' She sighed. 'But I do worry about her.'

'Rachel can take care of herself. She doesn't need her aunt checking up on her. And she is twenty-one, Mum.'

'I know. But with her mother away such a lot—'

Carey laughed. 'Oh, believe me, Mum, that suits Rachel just fine. You know they don't get on and apart from that, Aunt Marlene isn't about to be presented with any awards for Mother of the Year.'

Tayla grimaced. What Carey said was true. She couldn't deny that her older sister was not the best mother in the world. 'What did Rachel tell you about this guy anyway?'

Carey rolled her eyes and Tayla gave her a warning look. 'Not much,' she said with resignation. 'He's older, and absolutely gorgeous.'

'Well, I'm glad Rachel has invited him this weekend. I'd like to meet him.'

'Check him out, you mean. And I'm sure Rachel's bringing him along for just that reason,' Carey stated sardonically. 'Oh, and Rachel says he drives a sports car so he must be pretty rich.'

'A sports car doesn't mean he's rich,' Tayla put in.

'I know but he must be pretty well off because his family owns that big timber company, the one you're writing that article on for the weekend paper.'

'McCall's?' Kate frowned. 'The man I spoke to was sixty-ish. Duncan McCall. Maybe he was Rachel's boyfriend's father.'

'All I know is Rachel called him Mac.'

Kate suppressed a pang of concern. 'How much older than she is did Rachel say he was? You don't suppose—'

'Oh, give me a break, Mum! The old guy you talked to most likely has grandchildren and this Mac is probably one of them. Isn't the place called McCall and Sons?'

'Yes. But the company was started by Duncan McCall's father, although Duncan and his brother, Alex, run it now, so they're actually the sons.'

'Mum, cool it. I know you've looked after Rachel practically since she was born but she's all grown up. It's time now and it's called letting go.'

Tayla barely heard her daughter as she tried to recall everything she could about the interview she'd had with Duncan McCall. She was sure she would have remembered if he'd been at all flirtatious. She forced the frown from her face. 'I suppose Rachel is a sensible girl,' she said absently and Carey exclaimed in disgust.

'Exactly. You've got nothing to worry about where Rachel's concerned. At least *she* knows where it's at.'

'And is your tone saying, "Which is more than you can say for your aging mother"?'

'Right.' Carey laughed and then sighed theatrically, slouching in her seat belt. 'I'm more anxious about how I'm going to get through the weekend without being bored to death.'

'Did I mention that Nan's now on the Internet?' Tayla remarked casually and Carey sat bolt upright in her seat.

'No, you didn't. Since when?'

'I told you Nan was doing a computer users' course.'

'Yes, but I thought—'

'That Nan being an old woman she could only be exercising a flight of fancy? Well, she passed her course with flying colours and now she's got the bug. So you see, there should be plenty to interest you this weekend. I'm the one who may be bored to death by all the computer talk,' she added.

They completed the drive up the mountain with Carey waxing poetic on her favourite subject and Tayla was more than a little relieved to see the high iron fence that surrounded Nan's imposing house. She sighed as she turned between the ornate gates of the property that had been in her family for generations.

Auchnacree had been built by Tayla's great-grandfather before the turn of the century. He had painstakingly constructed the magnificent house, huge by any standards, for his bride and it was a wonderful example of the architecture of the time. That the materials had had to be brought up Mt. Tamborine by bullock dray only added to the romance of the story, one Nan loved to relate to new acquaintances. Tayla knew the story by heart and never tired of hearing it.

The lower floor of what was now referred to as a traditional Queenslander, was constructed of huge sandstone blocks and the floor areas under the upper verandas were covered by concrete ash pavers.

The upper floor was clad in timber and the steep-pitched roof was made of corrugated iron, while the iron on the roof of the wide verandas that surrounded the house was distinctively bull-nosed shaped. Cast-iron lace-work, featuring kangaroos and emus, adorned the upper verandas and wide wooden steps led up to the solid front door.

Tayla stopped the car under the shady boughs of a poinciana tree and as she looked up towards the house she smiled as she saw the large old Christmas wreath hanging on the front door. Nan had put that wreath on the front door each Christmas for as long as Tayla could remember.

A familiar blue Mitsubishi Lancer was parked on the driveway and Tayla raised her eyebrows in surprise. 'Looks like Rachel made it this afternoon after all.'

'Well, she told me she wouldn't be here.' Carey groaned. 'What am I supposed to say when she parades this guy anyway? "Oh, gee, Rachel, he sure is handsome." Or maybe, "And Mum thought you'd be sixty-four."'

'You dare, young lady, and Nan's computer is out of bounds.'

'You're a really cruel mother,' Carey quipped as she climbed from the car and opened the boot to hand out their overnight bags.

A dark-haired young woman came down the wide steps to greet them, hugging them both.

'Tayla. Carey. I made it today after all.'

That Rachel Dean was related to Tayla was obvious

although she was a little shorter and slimmer than her aunt. In fact, Rachel looked more like Tayla than Carey did. Carey was fair-haired like her late father while Rachel's hair was the same deep burnished auburn as Tayla's. However, whereas her aunt's was almost shoulder-length, Rachel's was cut and styled into a short cap that hugged her head.

'So where's the wonderful MacHandsome?' Carey asked without preamble and Rachel gave her a playful shove.

'I'm keeping you in suspense a bit longer.'

'We're looking forward to meeting him,' Tayla put in. 'Carey says you've been seeing him for some time.'

'Oh, not too long, actually,' Rachel said offhandedly.

'Is he tall? Dark? Handsome?' Carey teased and Rachel laughed.

'All of the above.'

'And rich?' Carey continued. 'Rich is always good.'

'Rich enough. And joke as much as you like, Carey. You'll think he's as dishy as I do. You, too, Tayla. You'll see.'

'I can hardly wait,' Carey commented dryly. 'So where is he?'

'Actually, I arrived early this morning. We came separately as he had to go into work for a few hours this morning. Later he wants to call in on a friend but he'll be here as soon as he can.' Rachel glanced at her watch. 'Any time now, I should think.'

They started up the wide wooden steps and Tayla ran her hand delicately along the carved railing. She loved this old house. It had first spiked her interest in old colonial homes.

'Here's my other two girls,' Nan exclaimed as she came through the open doorway.

Tayla hugged her grandmother, marvelling as she always did at how well Elizabeth Carey carried her eighty-eight years.

'Did you have a good trip up the mountain?' the older woman asked and Tayla nodded.

'Not much traffic so it was pretty good.'

Nan chuckled and patted Tayla's cheek. 'And I'm fine, so none of your mother duck look-overs. Apart from a bit of arthritis in my left knee, my old football wound, Dad used to call his, I'm as fit as a fiddle.'

Carey hugged her great-grandmother. 'Looking great, Nan. Happy birthday.'

'Thank you, love.' Nan kissed Carey's smiling cheek. 'And you get prettier every time I see you.'

Carey flushed. 'Rubbish, Nan. But what's this about you having a computer?'

'Carey!' Tayla protested but Nan pulled a face at her.

'Your mother's right, love. I'll show you my new toy later. We have to do the social stuff first.'

'Oh, right. Like meeting Rachel's Mr. MacWonderful.'

'I thought you were dying to meet him,' Rachel reminded her cousin sarcastically and Carey smirked.

'Well, Mum's looking forward to giving him the third degree,' Carey told her cousin with glee.

'He'll pass with flying colours.' Rachel grinned as she put her arm around her aunt and gave her a squeeze. 'Aunt Tayla, the mother hen.'

'I remember she used to wheel you around in her old pram when you were a baby while your great-grandfather had ten fits. And she changed your nappies so often your mother started complaining about the washing.'

'Enough of this,' Tayla begged and Rachel chuckled.

'Yes, now we're getting personal.'

'I never used to worry though,' Nan continued. 'You were a born mother even then. You should have had half a dozen children.'

'Oh, my God,' Carey said with feeling. 'Half a dozen rug-rats? Now we're talking a walking incubator.'

Tayla laughed to cover a pang of remembered sadness. She'd wanted at least two children but Mike, an only child with few relatives, hadn't been as interested in a family as she was.

It had been a source of contention between them when they were first married and with the surprise and unplanned arrival of Carey, Tayla had thought she'd change Mike's mind. But she hadn't.

Not that Mike hadn't loved his daughter. He had in his own serious way. As long as he didn't have to get too involved in the domestic side of parenthood.

And after Carey's birth he'd convinced Tayla that financially, they should concentrate on raising one child properly. But she would have loved to have had more children. Tayla pushed her memories out of her mind.

'Incubators, indeed!' Nan was saying. 'Oh, you young people. So open these days. I suppose it's an improvement on our times, though.' She shook her head. 'Let's go inside then.'

At that moment a throaty roar interrupted the parrots feeding in the native trees by the driveway. Flashes of green, red and orange splashed across the clear blue sky as the birds squawked in flight.

The growl of the engine grew louder and the four women turned towards the noise as a large black motorcycle rounded the curve in the driveway and drew to a halt just past the steps.

The rider was encased in black leather with vivid blue

stripes on his jacket and pants and helmet. Killing the engine, the man kicked the bike stand down and, with a sensuous grace, climbed off the huge machine. He slipped off his gloves and placed them on the seat before raising his hands to remove his helmet.

Longish dark hair clasped back in a ponytail escaped from the confines of his headgear and he turned a beard-roughened face towards them.

'Here's Rick now,' Rachel said and ran down the steps. 'Darling! You're here,' she said as she threw herself into his arms.

Tayla and Carey exchanged astonished glances and Tayla raised her eyebrows.

'Rick?' she queried softly. 'I thought his name was Mac.'

At that moment the tall man in question raised his dark head to look up at them. His vivid blue eyes met Tayla's and something shifted in her chest. She felt hot and then cold. And she was suddenly inexplicably and unfamiliarly breathless.

CHAPTER TWO

THE tall man stepped out of Rachel's embrace and took a small carryall from the pannier on the back of the motorcycle.

'Now that's a dashing young man,' Nan remarked in a whisper and Tayla frowned. 'If I were fifty years younger, well, I guess he wouldn't have been born.' She chuckled softly and Carey giggled.

The young man had stepped back from Rachel's embrace and at the sound of Nan's and Carey's laughter he turned to glance up at them again. His eyes fixed on Tayla, narrowed, yet she felt as though he had run his hands over her body. She shivered and stepped backwards, her hand going instinctively to the railing behind her.

Then Rachel was grabbing hold of the man's hand, drawing him forward and up the stairs.

As they approached, Tayla took an instinctive step backwards. For some reason she felt an almost overwhelming urge to turn and run. But run from what? She was being fanciful. Wasn't she?

Now they were all on the wide veranda and Rachel was making the introductions.

'Rick, this is my great-grandmother, Elizabeth Carey, my cousin, Carey Greer, and my aunt, Tayla Greer. Meet Rick McCall.'

'Mrs. Carey.' He inclined his dark head and bent over the thin hand the elderly woman held out to him.

'Pleased to meet you, Rick.' She dimpled with pleasure. 'And call me Nan. Everyone does.'

'Hi,' Carey said evenly as Rick flashed a smile at the young girl.

For once, Tayla realised, her daughter was showing neither aggression nor bravado. Obviously this man had passed muster with Carey.

'And Aunt Tayla.' Rick McCall's deep voice held a hint of humour yet the smooth, resonant tone set off that unfamiliar sinking in the pit of Tayla's stomach again and a small frown touched her brow.

Rachel was watching her aunt's face and she gave a nervous laugh. 'I think you can drop the *aunt* bit, Rick. Tayla's not much older than you are.'

Tayla glanced at the tall man again. Yes, he would be nearer thirty than Rachel's twenty-one years. Too old for her niece, surely? She swallowed a burst of misgivings. She was overreacting. This man was just a friend of Rachel's. It didn't mean her niece was going to marry him, regardless of Carey's intimations about bridesmaids earlier during their journey up the mountain.

Good manners had Tayla automatically holding out her hand. 'Nice to meet you, Mr. McCall,' she made herself say and her voice was almost steady.

He smiled then, showing a flash of strong white teeth, and, for long moments, his large hand folded firmly around hers. 'Likewise. And please, make it Rick.' He paused just slightly. 'Tayla.'

Tayla's eyes had settled involuntarily on the shape of his full lips and as he said her name her gaze shifted to meet his eyes. For long moments they looked at each other before Tayla made herself break that unsettling transitory contact.

'Well, let's all go on inside,' Nan was saying and

there was a general movement towards the open double leadlight doors.

Rick McCall politely stood back for the women to precede him.

'I've got a cup of tea brewing,' Nan continued, 'and I've just made some scones. You're in your usual rooms, girls, and I've put you in the blue room, Rick. Rachel will show you the way.'

'Thank you. And if you don't mind, Nan, I'll have a quick clean-up before I join you for a cuppa and your famous scones.'

'Famous?' Nan beamed at him. 'Oh, I'm afraid I'm not as good with my scones as my mother was.'

'That's not what I heard. Rachel told me they were delicious with your homemade strawberry jam.'

'Rachel always liked my jams.' Nan patted Rick's leather-clad arm. 'And you take as long as you like, Rick. Just unpack your bag and we'll all meet in the kitchen in the back.'

By then they were at the parting of the wide hallway and Rachel bore Rick off to the left while Tayla and Carey turned right. Nan hurried on towards the kitchen.

'Wow!' Carey exclaimed with feeling as she paused at her bedroom door and glanced at her mother. 'Is he a hunk or what? Mel Gibson eat your heart out! I didn't know Rachel had it in her to latch herself onto someone like that. I'm amazed. Totally amazed.'

'Carey.' Tayla made a half-hearted protest.

'Well, he is pretty gorgeous. And he is very Mel Gibson-ish, wouldn't you say, Mum?'

'Mmmm,' Tayla murmured non-committally as she went to walk on to the room next door.

'Just "Mmmm"?' Carey persisted. 'Mum, what's up? Don't you like him?'

'We've only just met him, Carey. I haven't known him long enough to know whether I like him or not.'

'I wasn't talking about his mind, Mum,' Carey said dryly. 'I meant his bod. And if you can't see that then our conversation this afternoon was a waste of my time. I don't need to worry about your sexual peak at all. It's been and gone.'

'Let's give that a rest, Carey. OK?'

Carey shrugged tolerantly. 'OK. But I bet he's all rippling muscles underneath that coating of black leather. And he rides a motorcycle. Cool.' She drew out the last word and Tayla reached for the doorknob.

'Cool he is,' she said evenly to waylay any further questions from her daughter before she stepped into her own room.

This bedroom with its high ceilings and pastel-shaded VJ walls had been hers since she and her older sister and brother had come to live here with Nan as children, orphaned when their parents had been accidentally killed. Yet today she barely gave the room's *olde-worlde* appointments a glance.

She crossed the polished wooden floor and set her overnight bag down on the carved wooden hope chest at the foot of the double-sized brass bed. Sinking onto the soft mattress, her hand rested on the brass knob on the bed end, her fingers absently tracing the white porcelain inserts. She felt all keyed up and fluttery in the stomach.

What was going on here? Was she coming down with something? she asked herself. She'd been perfectly all right on the trip up here. She bit her lip, loath to admit that this uneasiness had only started with Rick McCall's arrival.

Tayla shifted uncertainly and the springs in the old

bed creaked a little beneath her. What was her problem with Rick McCall? As she'd told Carey, she'd only just met the man. And Nan and Carey obviously hadn't taken a dislike to him.

Dislike. She turned the word over in her mind. Dislike. That wasn't quite what she meant. Disquiet. That was it. Rick McCall filled her with disquiet.

And somehow it had nothing to do with Rachel. The thought took her by surprise and she stood up quickly, turning to unzip her bag, taking out her hairbrush. Of course it was to do with Rachel, she told herself forcefully. She was simply concerned this man was suitable for her niece.

Tayla crossed to the dark, hand-carved dressing table and stood before the mirror, beginning to brush her hair. Her hand stilled. For the first time in ages she found her eyes moving assessingly over her face and body.

Her features were unremarkable, she told herself, not realising the combination of thick auburn hair that was inclined to curl, large green eyes and full curving lips gave her a subtle sensuousness that made both men and women take a second look.

As for her body, she was five feet nine and far from thin. Full-figured, she told herself mockingly. She had wide shoulders and a narrow waist and her rounded hips filled her denim jeans. Her breasts, also larger than was currently fashionable, thrust against her thin green cotton shirt and she noticed the second button from her collar had popped open, revealing the beginnings of her generous cleavage.

As Rachel made the introductions she'd caught Rick McCall's blue eyes flicking over her body. His gaze hadn't lingered suggestively the way she'd seen some men ogle her but she knew he'd looked her over for all that.

Simply reflex action, she told herself. Hadn't she glanced appraisingly at him? She knew he was tall, well over six feet, and that his legs were long and well-shaped, that his hips were narrow and his shoulders broad. In fact, he was, she had to acknowledge, a very attractive man.

And suddenly Tayla's breasts tingled, her nipples hardening, and a spiral of awareness began to shoot downwards. So much for Carey's dismissal of her waning sexual peak.

For heaven's sake! she berated herself, anyone would think— Tayla swallowed, her throat all at once dry. Was she physically attracted to this man? Angrily she drew the brush through her hair, the discomfort on her scalp making her blink. Attracted to Rick McCall? She was being ridiculous, she told herself. Totally and unequivocally ridiculous.

Rick McCall, she reminded herself, was Rachel's friend, to all outward appearances her own niece's boyfriend. Was she, Tayla, mad?

And as if that wasn't absurd enough, she continued to reprimand herself, Rick McCall wouldn't be interested in a well-built matron who was already going to seed. Tayla smiled self-disdainfully at her reflection, seeing herself as a flower, slightly past its first bloom, waving bravely from amidst a field of dewier blossoms.

All jesting aside, he was hardly her type anyway. Leathers. Long hair. Beard-roughened jaw. No, he was definitely not her style at all. He was nothing like Mike—

'Mum? You ready?' Carey stood in the doorway and Tayla turned to smile at her fair-haired daughter.

Now here was reality, Tayla Greer, she told herself. She was a thirty-four-year-old widow with a sixteen-year-old daughter and she'd do well to remember that.

'As ready as I'll ever be,' she replied lightly and followed Carey along the hallway towards the back of the house.

'Rick won't be long,' Rachel said as she breezed into the large homey kitchen and sat down beside her young cousin.

'Nice one, Rachel. What a hunk.' Carey took her cup of tea from her mother. 'MacHandsome he surely is.'

'MacHandsome?' Rachel giggled. 'He is all right, isn't he?'

'Handsome is as handsome does,' Nan put in. 'As long as he's pleasant and treats you well. Married life—'

'Hang on, Nan!' Rachel exclaimed with a laugh. 'Rick and I are just, well, friends,' she finished lamely, a blush colouring her young face.

Carey gave a disbelieving snigger. 'Friends? Oh, right. That's what they all say. You were all over him like a second skin when he arrived.'

'I hadn't seen him all day,' Rachel justified and Carey laughed again.

'Heaven help us if he'd been gone for a week. It would have been X-rated and Mum would have had to send me to my room quick-smart in case I was badly influenced and got the wrong idea.'

Rachel laughed, too. 'I suppose Rick does look sort of—' She paused.

'Deliciously bad,' Carey suggested and Rachel came to his defence.

'Rick's one of the nicest men I've ever met. He's kind and caring—'

'And sexy,' Carey added outrageously.

Rachel grinned. 'I guess so.'

'Sexy!' Nan tutted. 'I don't think you should talk about such things, Carey, at least not in front of your mother. You know what a prude she is.'

Rachel and Carey laughed delightedly as Tayla pursed her lips.

'Nan, I'm not a prude.'

'No, dear. If you say so.'

Was Nan just teasing? Tayla tried to gauge the expression on her grandmother's face. And was that how everyone saw her? Her daughter? Her niece? Tayla knew she liked order and a certain standard of behaviour, but, apart from that, she thought she was fairly easygoing.

'But Rachel's young beau is a very attractive man,' Nan was continuing. 'Don't you think so, Tayla?'

Tayla took a sip of her tea before answering. 'He is quite nice-looking if you like long hair and leathers.'

'Wicked!' Carey said with feeling and they all laughed again.

'He's a lot older than you are, Rachel,' Tayla said carefully and Rachel gave an exclamation of disgust.

'He's only twenty-eight and he's usually cleanshaven. Honest. He's been away you see, on holidays, so he's been relaxing.' Rachel frowned. 'You don't like him, do you, Tayla?'

'I don't know him,' Tayla began.

'But when you do get to know him, Tayla,' Rachel enthused, 'I promise you, you'll love him.'

'I have that effect on women,' said a deep voice from the doorway and they all swung around.

He was leaning casually on the doorjamb, his dark head almost reaching the lintel, and he seemed to fill the open space. His thumbs were tucked into the front belt loops of his clean blue jeans and one of his long legs was crossed over the other at the ankle.

He wore a pale blue denim shirt, the collar unbuttoned to reveal his strong tanned throat, the short sleeves hugging the well-developed biceps in his upper arms. His teeth flashed brightly against his dark jawline as he grinned in amusement.

Tayla's heartbeats did a decided flutter and her first thought was that her daughter had been right. Underneath the leather he *was* all muscle.

But how long had he been there? Had he heard their slightly suggestive conversation? He'd definitely heard Rachel's last remark to her aunt. *When you get to know him, Tayla, you'll love him.*

Rachel stood up and crossed to him and she gave him an affectionate shove. 'I was going to say something about eavesdroppers never hearing good of themselves but I can't really say that because we were all singing your praises.'

'All of you?' Rick asked lightly and his blue eyes, narrowing mockingly, met Tayla's. 'I'm overcome and feeling a little fraudulent.'

Rachel's laugh was a little forced. 'Fraudulent? Don't be silly, Rick. Come on in and join us.'

He crossed to the table and sat down where Rachel indicated. Nan passed him his tea.

'Thanks, Nan,' he said easily. 'You have a wonderful home here.'

Nan beamed and gave him a short history of *Auchnacree*. Tayla listened even though she'd heard the story a hundred times before. She could almost hear the crack of the whip, see the slow, heavy plod of the bullocks carting the large sandstone blocks and what timber wasn't available on site.

She glanced up to see Rick McCall watching her and she looked away, embarrassed that he might have seen the dreamy expression on her face.

'Rick's something of an expert on old houses, aren't you, Rick?' Rachel said enthusiastically. 'He runs the Heritage Unit at McCall's. If anyone wants advice on anything to do with renovating old buildings they consult Rick.'

'Then how come you didn't get to talk to Mum last month when she was researching her story on McCall's?' Carey echoed Tayla's own thoughts.

'You're a journalist?' Rick turned to Tayla and she shrugged.

'I do some freelance work. I spoke to Duncan McCall,' she said lightly. 'And, come to think of it, to a younger man. David McCall, I think. His son?' Tayla raised her eyebrows inquiringly and Rick nodded.

'Yes. Duncan's my uncle and David is my cousin.'

Subconsciously Tayla noticed Rachel's cheeks were slightly pink and she was giving the contents of her cup earnest scrutiny.

'Your uncle gave me a brief outline of your family's company,' she continued. 'About James McCall coming out from Scotland, starting the business and building it into one of the few large family-owned businesses left in the city.'

Rick smiled. 'My maternal grandmother knew James and his wife well, and she said James was a canny old devil, as tight with his money as they come, but a great businessman.'

'Duncan McCall did say he had a brother and a nephew also involved in the company, apart from his own two sons.' Tayla paused, her conversation with Duncan McCall coming back to her.

She had an interview with a Patrick McCall on Tuesday afternoon. She was almost sure Duncan McCall had said Patrick was his nephew. Was that Rick's brother? Patrick. Wasn't Rick a derivative of the name Patrick? They had to be the same person. She must have an interview with this man. Tayla swallowed as realisation dawned.

'And do you have any siblings?' she asked, already knowing the answer.

'Two older sisters who aren't involved in the business.'

'So you're the nephew who was away on leave, the one who usually dealt with the Heritage side of the business.' Tayla put the last piece of the puzzle into place.

Rick nodded again. 'That's me. My father, Alex, and my uncle, Duncan, handle the day-to-day side of the timber yard with Duncan's elder son, Royce, managing the shipping section. Royce's younger brother, David, is more in sales and promotion.'

'David travels a lot,' Rachel began and stopped. She exchanged a look with Rick and then she flushed a little. 'I feel like I know all about the family from Rick. But Rick's usually there,' she finished quickly and Tayla suspected Rachel had revised what she had started to say.

'So you've been on holiday?' Nan put in to the short silence and Rick nodded.

'I went touring up to north Queensland and the Daintree. It's a beautiful area up there in the north.'

They discussed various national parks although Tayla didn't add a lot to the conversation. She kept dwelling on her proposed interview with Rick McCall on Tuesday. Should she cancel it? Or would that look too pointed?

And then Carey was bringing the subject around to her obsession.

'So are you computerised?' she asked Rick and he laughed.

'Not personally.'

Carey grinned. 'I meant McCall's, the company. What sort of software do you use? At work,' she added distinctly.

'Carey,' Tayla appealed, reprimanding her daughter but Rick waved his hand.

'It's okay. Actually, I've been trying to convince Dad and my uncle to change systems.' He turned to Carey and they began a complicated and complex conversation that totally bewildered Tayla.

She sipped her tea, letting the sound of Rick McCall's deep voice wash over her. His deep tones were mellow and fluid and Tayla couldn't recall ever wanting to just sit and enjoy the sound of anyone's voice.

'Perhaps I could have a look at it one day,' Carey was saying. 'Maybe I could come with Mum when she goes over for her follow-up interview for her story. Can I, Mum?'

Tayla came slowly out of her preoccupation with Rick McCall's voice and she flushed. 'I'm sorry. What was that, love?'

'I was wondering if I could come with you when you go back to McCall's?' Carey repeated and Rick's dark brows rose.

'What sort of story are you writing?' he asked and Tayla gave a soft cough, trying to pull her thoughts together.

'I saw your uncle a few weeks ago. It's part of a series I'm doing on historical houses in and around Brisbane. When I was talking to the owners of the last home I featured they mentioned that the staff at McCall's were indispensable when it came to advice and service. So I'm incorporating McCall's into the series. With your uncle's permission, of course.'

'You must have been away when Tayla was there, Rick,' Rachel said and Tayla saw a strange look pass between Rachel and her boyfriend.

'What publication do you write for and when does your article come out?' Rick asked.

'The Saturday supplement of the *Courier Mail* and the one featuring McCall's will be in the weekend edition the week after next.'

'I'll be interested to read it and the previous articles,' Rick said easily. 'I'm sure my uncle will have kept copies for our Heritage file.'

'If he didn't we've got them at home,' Carey told him. 'Mum can photocopy them for you. She has copies of all her articles.'

'Which particular houses have you written about?' Rick persisted and Tayla shifted uncomfortably.

She mentioned the three homes that had already been featured in her six-week series. 'I've done *Dunsmara* for this week and then we'll put in the piece on McCall's. For the one after that I'm hoping to do *Meadowmont* if I can contact the owners.' She gave a grimace. 'They're proving a little difficult to reach.'

'Ah, yes.' Rick nodded. '*Meadowmont*. That's a wonderful home, built around 1860. Bob and Jenny Ainscough own it. I know them quite well. They've done a wonderful job on the restorations. One of the best I've seen.'

'Maybe Rick could set it up for you,' Rachel suggested and Tayla shook her head.

'Oh, I wouldn't want to put him to the trouble,' she

protested, overcoming her urge to press for the offer. The Ainscoughs hadn't returned her calls and she wished she could hand Rick McCall her mobile phone and get him to ring his friends on the spot. A true journalist wouldn't have hesitated, but—

'It's no trouble,' Rick said easily. 'I'll get your phone number before I leave and have Bob or Jenny contact you.'

Rachel beamed at him. 'There you are, Tayla. It's all arranged.'

The conversation turned to other matters and soon Rachel was standing up, intent on showing Rick over the family property, as she referred to the house and its adjacent orchards.

Carey and Nan only needed Rachel and Rick to leave the kitchen and they announced they were going to have a play on Nan's new computer. They belatedly asked Tayla to join them but she declined, saying she was a little tired and thought she might relax and do a little reading.

Tayla returned to her room to collect her book and then headed out onto the back veranda. She levered herself onto the rope hammock stretched across from the wall to the veranda post and picked up her book. It was a mystery best-seller she'd been trying to find time to read and this seemed an ideal opportunity.

She could hear Nan and Carey talking computers in the study nearby. Lazily she glanced at the cover of her book but didn't immediately open it. Instead her gaze moved over the scene from the high veranda. This was the best view from the house, she considered.

The sky was that clear crisp blue that almost hurt your eyes and for once there was little haze over the valley. The trees were a carpet of smoky green stretching below, the colour broken only occasionally by the outcrops of tawny rocks. To Tayla's left, clinging to a rocky bluff and only partially visible was the house of their nearest neighbour, a well-known Queensland writer.

Tayla sighed, entranced by the view, and yet, all at once, she felt slightly melancholy again. She admonished herself irritably. She had no reason to be despondent. Her life was going along quite nicely now after those first few years of emotional turmoil after Mike died.

She'd continued with her job teaching at a private and very prestigious girls' school and she was doing well with her journalism course. She'd had quite a deal of success with her freelance articles and this current series on Brisbane's historical houses had been a real coup. The editor had even tentatively agreed to her ideas for a second series on the lesser known houses, the many quaint and attractively restored workers' cottages that clustered close to the Central Business District of the city.

Apart from an occasional minor hiccup she shared a good relationship with her daughter. Life was rosy, she told herself. But lonely. The thought crept up on her, slithered under her guard, and she shifted in the hammock, making it swing gently.

Lonely? Ridiculous! Tayla almost laughed at herself. What with Carey, her job, her writing and her studies she had no spare time to be lonely.

Of course, she missed Mike but— Well, she acknowledged guiltily, that had settled over time and although she often thought of him she didn't continuously dwell on his loss.

With a faint exclamation of vexation she deliberately

opened her book and spent the rest of the afternoon involved in its complicated plot.

For once the downy comfort of the familiar old brass bed didn't soothe Tayla when she climbed into bed that night. For some reason she couldn't sleep and the night seemed to be closing in on her. Old memories crowded in with the darkness and she found herself thinking of Mike.

They'd met at high school, had their first official date when she was sixteen and he was almost eighteen. Just over two years later they had married with only grudging permission from Nan.

For some reason Nan had never completely taken to the tall and fair young man Tayla wanted to marry but she had acknowledged Mike had genuinely cared for Tayla.

Looking back, Tayla could see that Mike's somewhat dour nature was probably responsible for Nan's apprehension. Mike did have a tendency to take himself very seriously. While Nan enjoyed nothing more than a good laugh.

Their plan, Mike's and hers, when they had married, had been for Tayla to keep working until Mike had finished his degree. And then Tayla had discovered she was pregnant with Carey, a honeymoon baby, and those careful plans had had to be revised.

At first Mike had been angry, repeating his resolution that he didn't care for children, that he hadn't wanted any. At least not until they had made their way in the world, meaning that he was qualified, had bought a house, a decent car and had settled into a secure job. Tayla's assurances that she would work as long as she could, and would then return to work as soon as possible had reconciled some of his concern.

And fortunately it had all worked out in the end. Not long after Carey was born Mike had landed a part-time job with a reputable firm and they had taken him on when he graduated. In the almost ten years he was with them he had steadily worked his way up to a managerial position and when he'd died he was about to be offered a partnership.

Mike had been overjoyed at that. Much to Tayla's dismay he'd talked excitedly about moving to another house, a better house in a better suburb. At the time Tayla was gradually renovating their home, bringing it back to the former glory it had enjoyed when it was first built nearly a century ago. She was proud of her achievements and loved the pretty little cottage with its well-established gardens.

But fate had stepped in and Mike was gone before they could even begin discussing the merits of moving house. He'd left for work one morning as usual and been killed in a freak traffic accident. A truck carrying heavy steel cables had jackknifed on Coronation Drive and Mike's car had been crushed by the shifting load. Mike was rushed to the nearby hospital but hadn't regained consciousness. Tayla had known him for nearly twenty years and then he was gone.

She brought his face into her mind's eye. His fair hair had begun to thin and turn prematurely grey and his face always seemed to be set in serious lines, as though he had the weight of the world on his shoulders. But he'd been a good husband and she'd loved him. In the beginning he'd been a rather distant father but once Carey had grown from babyhood into a talking little person he had grown closer to her.

Their marriage may not have set the world on fire but it had been steady and secure and she did miss him. In the five years since his death she hadn't really been interested in getting involved in another relationship. In fact she couldn't recall contemplating re-entering the world of dating and all it entailed, even if there had been anyone she'd noticed.

And suddenly Rick McCall's face sprang into her mind. Tayla's eyes opened wide in surprise. What had made her think of that particular man? She shifted disconcertedly in the bed and the springs creaked softly.

Rick's craggy face stayed with her, vividly tangible, his jaw shaded and unshaven, his striking blue eyes meeting hers with their confusing, perturbing message.

There was no message, she told herself exasperatedly. He was simply a man who must enjoy the admiring attention of women because he was, she had to admit, an extremely attractive man. He had the kind of features that would always warrant a second look.

Tayla could see what had charmed Rachel. That rugged, unkempt appearance held a hint of danger, of forbidden and risky territory. Tayla could understand women, young women, being drawn to him and all that his outward mien promised. He was certainly a man to fit all fantasies.

She shivered slightly, feeling an almost forgotten sensation in her lower stomach. But forgotten or not, she knew exactly what the feeling meant and she was horrified at herself.

She'd never been attracted to Rick McCall's type of man. The idea that she could be intrigued by his rugged good looks mixed with that hint of smouldering sensuality was a total anathema. And this frisson of purely sexual arousal was alien to her. And it frightened her.

She preferred, was used to, the comfort and security of Mike's undemanding temperament. In all the years she was married to Mike she'd never considered looking elsewhere for any sort of sexual experience. And if the earth had never moved for her then she had reconciled herself to the fact that neither she nor Mike were of a particularly sexual nature.

Or was it simply that she had buried that specific side of her personality because Mike had subtly led her to believe it was abhorrent to him? Where had that thought come from? she demanded of herself and then grew agitated because she knew she didn't want an answer to the question.

In a burst of self-disgust Tayla climbed from the bed and crossed to the door. The wooden floorboards were cool beneath her bare feet until she stepped into the hallway and onto the carpet runner. With one hand on the wall to guide her she moved through the dimness towards the kitchen.

Perhaps a cup of tea would settle her down. Coffee would only compound the problem. She'd already been staring at the ceiling for hours.

Tayla had stepped into the kitchen before she realised there was a faint glow in the darkness.

'Don't move,' said a deep voice, and she froze, her breath catching in her throat.

CHAPTER THREE

TAYLA'S brain told her to scream but when she opened her mouth nothing ventured forth. A cold hand seemed to clutch at her vocal cords and her knuckles turned white where she'd automatically gripped the doorframe.

'I mean, don't move, please,' said that same deep voice, this time with a hint of humour. 'I dropped some grapes and I haven't rounded them all up yet.'

The tall figure opened the refrigerator door a little wider and the interior light changed the intensity of the shadows, threw his dark face into eerie angles.

Tayla took a calming breath and her gaze swept the length of his body. He was bare-footed as she was, and he wore only his jeans, slung low on his narrow hips. His chest was bare and Tayla couldn't seem to drag her eyes from the dark contours of his tanned skin, the beautiful symmetry of his well-defined muscles, the light matt of hair on his chest that arrowed down to his waist, to disappear beneath the waistband of his jeans. And her breathing refused to settle.

She made herself take a shallow breath as she stepped shakily forward, only to give a startled gasp as something wet squelched between her bare toes.

'Ugh!' Tayla exclaimed, lifting her foot from the squashed fruit.

'Oh, no.' Rick McCall swung the fridge door wide. 'I suspect you found one of the rogue grapes. Perhaps I should drop some more and we could start our own label.'

'Label?' Tayla repeated, feeling for a paper towel on the countertop.

'Vino,' he explained and his white teeth flashed in his dark face. 'Greer-McCall White Label, hmmm?'

'Oh.' Tayla swabbed at the gooey mess. 'No, thanks. It feels revolting.'

'Stay still. Help is at hand.' He crossed the kitchen, put the bowl of grapes on the table and grabbed another paper towel. Then he went down on his haunches in front of her, took her bare foot in his hand and proceeded to wipe her toes.

And suddenly Tayla began to grow hot where his cool fingers touched her skin. The heat spread, suffused her body and a tingle began in the pit of her stomach. She pulled her foot from his hand.

'Thank you,' she got out as he turned his attention to the mess on the floor.

'No worries. It was my fault for sneaking in here for a midnight snack.' He stood up, his lithe body uncurling, leaving him standing far too close to Tayla for her comfort.

She moved backwards, crossed her arms over the front of her nightshirt, in case he saw the swollen peaks of her breasts as they stood to attention beneath the thin cotton. Her eyes were on the level of his chin and if she leaned forward just a little her lips would rest in the hollow of his strong throat. Tayla's mouth went dry.

'Do you think it's true what they say?' Rick was asking and Tayla blinked as her mind tried to catch up with his words.

'About...about what?' she said thickly.

'Stolen fruit. Being sweeter.' He turned slightly and chose a grape from the bowl on the table, slipped it between his lips. 'Want one?'

One what? The question screamed inside Tayla. One touch of her lips on his cool skin? One lingering kiss on his incredible mouth? She almost moaned in horror. What was wrong with her?

'No.' The word burst out of her and she swallowed. 'No, thanks,' she repeated a little more evenly. 'I just wanted a—' She swallowed again. 'A drink.' She went to move towards the sink.

'How about some tea? Now that you mention it I could use a cuppa myself.' He leaned forward, invading Tayla's space once again, and she had to stop herself jumping away from him. But he was simply reaching for the light switch and the kitchen was bathed in brightness.

Tayla blinked, turned to reach for the kettle, as her eyes adjusted to the light. It was little defence against his seeing and recognising her agitation. She had to get away from him, get herself under control.

He stepped after her, completely disconcerting her, and her eyes flew to meet his in concern. But he was simply reaching across to take the kettle from her.

'I'll do that while you find the tea-leaves. I've got no idea where Nan keeps them,' he said easily.

Tayla watched him as he leaned over the sink, his broad shoulders gleaming under the artificial light. She had to admit he had the most beautiful body she'd ever seen. Or at least, that she'd noticed.

And when was the last time she'd so much as glanced at a man's body? she asked herself. She had no ready answer. She tried to think about Mike, what he'd looked like, and she shifted uneasily.

Mike hadn't been a very physical person. He would never have walked around without a shirt. He had even dressed in the small dressing room off their bedroom. And he'd always worn pyjamas to bed, would never have had to slip on a pair of jeans over his nakedness if he had to get up and raid the kitchen for a midnight snack.

Yet, early in their marriage, hadn't they, she and Mike, snuggled naked in the darkness? She was sure they had. They must have. But they certainly hadn't since Carey was born.

'I was lying in bed absolutely starving,' Rick was saying as he filled the kettle. 'Rachel and I had dinner with some friends of mine. Diedre, Mark's wife, is a gourmet cook but she's into what I call designer food. Looks very pleasing on the eye, beautifully presented on octagonal plates, but not exactly hale and hearty stuff. Even with dessert my rumbling tummy kept me awake.' He grinned over his shoulder. 'I didn't think Nan would mind if I had a small snack to tide me over till breakfast.'

'No. Of course she wouldn't mind,' Tayla put in politely.

'So what woke you up? Not Rachel and I coming home, was it?' Rick asked easily.

'Woke me up?' Tayla dragged her disquieting thoughts back to the conversation. 'Oh, no. You didn't wake me. I haven't been asleep, I don't think. I sometimes get like this. Start thinking and then can't relax my conscious mind. At home I usually get up and do some work but—' Tayla stopped and looked up to see him watching her, his arms folded over his bare chest.

She turned away and lifted the canister holding Nan's tea-leaves down from the shelf.

'I have that trouble, too. More so lately,' he added softly as he reached for the teapot. He took the canister from Tayla and spooned the tea-leaves into the pot, his dark hair, free from its confining band, shimmering in dark waves that almost reached his shoulders.

Tayla stood on the other side of the scrubbed wooden table and fought an almost irresistible urge to move around to join him, to run her hands over his smooth skin, move her fingers in his thick dark hair. Instead she subsided onto a chair, afraid her suddenly weak knees would give way beneath her.

They watched in silence as the kettle began to whistle and then Rick was pouring boiling water onto the tea-leaves and reaching for two fine china tea mugs from the dresser.

'Black, one sugar, wasn't it?' he asked as he set the teapot on the table.

'Yes.' He had a good memory. He must have noticed how she drank her tea when she'd had her second cup this afternoon. Tayla watched him pour the aromatic liquid into her cup and then add a spoonful of sugar. He seemed as at home in this very domestic setting as he was astride his powerful motorcycle.

When he set her tea carefully on the table Tayla wrapped her hands around the mug, trying to encourage the heat on her palms to distract her from Rick McCall's tall figure across the width of the table from her.

'There's some cake in the tin on the counter behind you,' she said as evenly as she could.

Rick turned and opened the lid. 'This looks good,' he said and took a knife from the cutlery drawer, cutting himself a generous slice. 'Want some?' he offered and Tayla shook her head.

She was going to be flat out swallowing her tea, let alone eating a slice of cake. She took a careful sip of her drink, setting the mug back on the tabletop as Rick sat down opposite her.

'This is great,' he said, indicating the slice of cake. 'Did Nan make it?'

'Ah, no. I did,' Tayla admitted reluctantly and he grinned again.

He went to comment and then changed his mind, his strong white teeth biting off another mouthful of cake. 'I'll bet Nan taught you how to make it though,' he said when he'd swallowed the cake.

Tayla managed a tight smile. Her attention had been caught by the movement of the muscles in his throat as he swallowed and she drew her eyes away, made herself concentrate on the dark liquid in her mug. 'Yes, Nan did teach me to cook. That's one of the family's favourite recipes. She taught Rachel to cook, too,' Tayla added, reminding herself of her niece's relationship with this man.

Rick's blue eyes seemed to be studying what remained of his cake. 'I'll have to get her to make me one,' he said lightly and an uncomfortable silence echoed about them, a heavy stillness that seemed to be burdened by a multitude of unspoken thoughts.

Tayla drew herself together, her hands still gripping her cup for support. Although why she found herself needing tangible assistance she couldn't quite explain to herself.

But the silence was becoming intolerable to her. She had to break it, bring some normality to the situation.

'It sounded as though you enjoyed your visit to the Daintree,' she said tentatively and he nodded.

Was he equally relieved to settle into an ordinary topic of conversation? Or was she being fanciful?

'Yes. The Daintree's an incredible heritage that we need to protect. The feel, the sounds of the rainforest are indescribable.'

'And did you get out to the Great Barrier Reef at all?' This wasn't so difficult, Tayla conceded. She just had to keep everything, including her capricious thoughts, in order.

'A couple of times,' Rick was replying. 'I spent a week with friends who own a resort out from Airlie Beach in the Whitsundays. Craven Island. A truly beautiful place. Have you heard of it?'

Tayla nodded in surprise. 'Carey and I had two weeks there just last year. It was amazing. You know the Denisons?'

'Ryan and Liv? Sure do. I did some consulting on some refurbishment they did a few years ago. They're a great family.'

Tayla smiled. 'Carey made friends with the twins. In fact she still writes to Melanie and I think she had a crush on young Luke at the time.'

She took another sip of her tea and found herself suddenly remembering the uneasiness she'd felt when she'd compared her relationship with Mike with the wonderful rapport that seemed to exist between Ryan Denison and his wife, Liv. On Craven Island she'd experienced the same uneasiness that Rick McCall caused inside her. And yet not quite the same. Had that been the beginning of her restlessness, her questioning of the direction of her life?

Tayla frowned unconsciously. What was wrong with her? She was perfectly happy with her life. Wasn't she? And until now she hadn't been questioning anything. Apart from that, there was absolutely no point in examining her marriage and finding it wanting. Not then and certainly not now.

It was simply too late at night and she should be in bed asleep rather than dallying in the kitchen with Rachel's boyfriend. Tayla stood up.

'Well, thanks for the tea. I should get to sleep now.'

Fat chance, she told herself. She felt more unsettled now than she had before she left her room.

Rick paused as he took a sip of his own tea, looked across at her, and his dark lashes fell to shield his expression.

Tayla picked up her almost empty cup and then sensed his eyes flick over her. Involuntarily she looked up, saw his gaze linger momentarily on her breasts, unrestrained beneath her cotton nightshirt. The material was hardly transparent but she felt as though he'd reached out and actually touched her. And, with a mixture of astonishment and abhorrence, she had to acknowledge the feeling was a very long way from being unpleasant.

Her nipples hardened and she went to move quickly around the table, to make her escape. In her haste she caught her foot on the table leg and felt herself falling.

She clutched at the tabletop to save herself but Rick McCall was on his feet, his hand on her arm, steadying her. Somehow Tayla also managed to avoid the splash of hot tea dregs left in her mug.

Once she had her balance her attention went to Rick's strong fingers still encircling her arm. His hand was cool and firm and her skin tingled where it touched her. If she hadn't been holding her mug she knew her other hand would now be resting on his broad chest and her mouth went dry at the mere thought.

'I'm sorry,' she got out a little breathlessly. 'I must be more tired than I thought I was.'

Slowly his fingers released her and he stepped back, putting some space between them. 'Did you hurt your foot?' He was looking down and Tayla gathered herself together.

'No. It's fine.' She took the couple of steps toward

the sink to prove her point, rinsed her cup and set it on the drainer. 'I'll…I'll see you in the morning.'

'Sure,' he replied lightly.

With a sigh of relief Tayla crossed to the doorway and slipped out into the darkness of the hallway. Yet she couldn't prevent herself looking back at him. He'd returned to his seat and seemed to be gazing down at what remained of his own tea in the cup in his hand.

Tayla moved slowly and quietly along the hallway to her room, grateful when she had closed the door behind her. She slid into bed and pulled the sheet up to her neck, her fingers clutching it there in unconscious protection.

Now in the safety of her room she could analyse her reaction to Rick McCall's hand on her arm. And why she had been so distressed by that innocent touch. It had been an automatic movement on his part, to prevent her falling over the table, a table she told herself she'd been familiar with all her life. How she'd come to misjudge the length of it she didn't know.

Oh, dear God! What was wrong with her?

Her mouth went dry as a thought hit her like a bolt of lightning. She was disoriented because of her attraction to Rick McCall. No! She wasn't— Was she? She rubbed her hands over her tired eyes. Well, she couldn't be. That was the end of the story. Rick McCall was way out of bounds.

He was her own niece's friend. No, not friend. He was Rachel's boyfriend. She had to remember that. And if that wasn't enough, Rick McCall was so much younger than she, Tayla, was. Even leaving Rachel out of the equation, that fact made the situation insurmountable. Hadn't she criticised her own sister for such inappropriate behaviour?

Tayla swallowed as her thoughts went to Marlene. Her sister was eight years older than Tayla and, at twenty, Marlene had married a wealthy grazier, Rachel's father, who was almost twenty years her senior. That marriage had lasted barely five years before they were divorced. With a more than reasonable settlement Marlene had returned home, bringing Rachel to stay with Nan and Tayla. Marlene had then headed off alone on a tour of Europe.

Since then they had been lucky to see her once a year. Husband number two was the heir of a wealthy French entrepreneur. He was three years younger than Marlene's thirty years. A divorcee again at thirty-nine, Marlene had married a handsome twenty-two-year-old, a marriage that had lasted little more than twelve months.

Marlene's latest marriage, and Marlene was now almost forty-three, was to a successful English businessman who, Marlene had told Tayla, was yet to see forty. Her sister and new brother-in-law were having an extended honeymoon in Venice over Christmas and Marlene had half promised they'd visit in the new year.

Tayla loved her sister but she knew she didn't approve of her behaviour, beginning with her cavalier attitude to her daughter, Rachel. And as far as the younger men were concerned, Tayla rather suspected she had had a holier than thou opinion of that kind of conduct.

When Marlene had married the twenty-two-year-old Tayla's concern had been for Rachel and how her niece would see this mismatched union. Rachel had simply shrugged while Tayla had been criticism personified. She and Marlene had had a trans-Atlantic argument via the telephone, resulting in the sisters not speaking to each other for some months.

Now, it seemed, Tayla was no better than her sister.

Perhaps it ran in their genes, she reflected wryly. No, said an inner voice, it had more to do with Rick McCall's jeans. Tayla bit off a laugh, suspecting she was growing just slightly hysterical with the turmoil her reflections were creating.

Well, she told herself forcefully, she didn't have to be like Marlene and act on such fantasies. For that was all they were. Pure fantasies. And the operative point was she didn't have to take this momentary lapse in judgment any further. And she certainly wasn't going to.

Tayla told herself she had had a happy and stable marriage and if Mike hadn't been killed she would still be happily married and this problem would never have arisen.

Or would it? The doubt crept relentlessly in. Hadn't her marriage been happy simply because she had settled on her lot and made it so? Hadn't she recognised that her life with Mike was boring and a little stifling and that she'd taken on her course in journalism to give her an outside interest that was apart from Mike and his ultraconservative predisposition?

But no, she told herself guiltily. Her marriage hadn't been that bad. Stable didn't necessarily mean boring. And sedate and well-adjusted adults didn't accede to brief flashes of attraction. They recognised them for what they were and got on with their lives, faced their responsibilities.

Yet just for that one moment in the kitchen Tayla knew the last thing she wanted to be was well-adjusted and sensible. Just then she'd wanted desperately to be wild and abandoned.

She took an unsteady breath. She was being absolutely ridiculous. She turned over and closed her eyes, willing herself to find the oblivion of slumber. She closed her mind and tried to concentrate on her usual method of falling off to sleep.

It was as though she played a video in her mind, picturing a long white beach, green-topped palm trees, crystal-clear turquoise water washing gently on the sand. She could almost hear the rustle of the breeze in the palm leaves, the constant song of the water washing the shore, the soft crunch of bare feet on damp sand. And there she was strolling along the water's edge, her feet lapped by the cool water.

Usually when she concentrated on this picture she slipped into dreamless sleep but tonight the whole perspective seemed to have changed. A second figure joined her, a tall, dark-haired figure, with broad, well-defined shoulders and narrow hips. He took her hand and pulled her to him and his lips claimed hers. And try as she may, she couldn't, or wouldn't, bring the shadowy figure into focus.

Dawn was lightening the sky when she finally drifted into a troubled sleep.

'If you come with me you'll have to entertain yourself while I conduct the interview,' Tayla told her daughter. 'I mean, I won't be able to leave if you get bored.'

'You know, I think you think I'm spoiled,' Carey remarked indignantly. 'How long do you expect this interview to take anyway?'

'I don't know till I get there.' Or how I'll feel seeing Rick McCall again, Tayla added to herself.

Carey shrugged. 'Then I'll talk to Rick.'

'I think it'll be Rick McCall I'll be talking to,' Tayla said, not looking at her daughter.

'It will? You didn't say anything about that at the weekend.' Carey frowned. 'Why didn't you?'

'Well, I wasn't sure. But if he's in charge of the Heritage Unit then it stands to reason he'll be the one I should talk to.'

'Oh.' Carey thought about that. 'I guess you're right. Well, maybe Rick will let me look at his computer.'

'I don't think that's likely, love. McCall's is a multi-million-dollar business. They're not going to let you play around with their computer system.'

'Play around?' Carey stuck her hands on her hips. 'Mother, that's insulting. Didn't they tell you at the Parent-Teacher night that your little darling, namely me, was a computer genius of the highest order? And I never play around with computers, however it may look to the uninitiated observer.'

'That's not what it looks like when those little people march along the screen digging and climbing and blowing things up.'

'Those little people are lemmings and I admit I occasionally take recreational breaks. But it's still not playing around,' Carey insisted.

'All right. I apologise if I insulted your fragile adolescent ego.'

Carey expelled a noisy breath.

'But,' Tayla continued, 'I still don't care for you touching the McCall's computers. Even if Rick McCall gives his permission.'

'Is it okay if I ask questions?' Carey rolled her eyes exasperatedly. 'Or do I have to be seen and not heard?'

'That works for me,' Tayla said lightly. 'So if you're coming with me you'd better hustle because I'm leaving in ten minutes max.'

Carey sighed theatrically. 'On second thoughts I think I'll stay home.'

'Suit yourself.' Tayla guiltily swallowed a rush of relief. In all honesty she preferred to face this interview with Rick McCall without having her attention divided. She had enough to think about without having to worry about the possibility of her daughter throwing the McCall's computer system into disarray. 'I guess I should be going then.'

'You're wearing that?' Carey asked and Tayla looked down at her plain navy skirt and matching short-sleeved shirt-jacket.

'What's wrong with this?'

'It makes you look, well—' Carey frowned. 'I don't know. Sort of matronly.'

'Matronly?' Tayla repeated. 'I thought I was power dressing.'

'It's the colour. It's too dark. What about that outfit you bought last week?'

Tayla frowned. 'The bright green one? I've had second thoughts about that. I think it may have been a mistake. Besides, darker colours make me look slimmer.'

'Rubbish!' Carey stated emphatically. 'You're not fat. The green one would suit your colouring better. Or at least wear the brighter blue one. That colour's too bland.'

Tayla wavered. 'I'm only going to ask questions, not apply for a job.'

'I'm just thinking you should be prepared, Mum. You never know who you might see. What if you meet a guy who really turns you on and you want to impress him and you're not looking your best? What then?'

'That scenario is highly unlikely,' Tayla said dryly. 'At the risk of sounding cynical I haven't met a guy who—' she grimaced '—turns me on, in years.'

Liar! Liar! jeered a small voice inside her. Wasn't she

going to interview the only man to attract her since Mike died?

'And if I do I intend to run very quickly in the opposite direction. As I told you before, I don't need those kinds of complications at the moment,' Tayla finished forcefully, hoping she'd take heed of her firmly stated words.

'Give me strength!' Carey appealed to the room in general. 'Let's have a look at your gear.' She opened her mother's old-fashioned wardrobe and pulled out a lightweight cotton suit in a peacock blue colour. 'This one I think. It makes your eyes sort of green-blue like the sea. Trust me on this, Mum. This would be better than the navy one.'

Tayla sighed and unbuttoned her top. It was easier to concede defeat. Who cared what she wore anyway, as long as it was cool, for as Christmas approached, the summer heat was relentless.

With a vague sense of nervousness Tayla drove over to the timber company and turned into the parking lot, guiding the car into a space between two utes that had seen better days. She went to check her hair and makeup in the rear vision mirror but stopped herself in irritation. There was no reason to make an inspection. She knew she was neat and tidy.

Butterflies fluttered in her stomach as she climbed from the car into the searing heat of the sun. She'd locked the car before she realised she'd left her briefcase inside on the passenger seat.

Pull yourself together, she admonished herself as she retrieved the case and relocked the car. She strode purposefully across to the entry, sighing with relief as the automatic doors closed behind her and she was in the air-conditioned building.

As Christmas was approaching the ceilings and shelves were festooned with sparkling tinsel and intricate and colourful paper decorations. Soft Christmas carols played in the background and Santa Claus's smiling face suggested various gift ideas. Enticing-looking gaily-wrapped boxes with huge bows added to the seasonal ambience.

The huge complex was a dream for tradesman and handyman alike. To the left was the basic hardware and timber section while to the right was a replica colonial worker's cottage displaying all manner of period joinery. Tayla knew this marked the Heritage section, a must-visit for anyone renovating an old home or building.

On display were various timber shapes and sizes in fretwork, dowels, railings and doors and there were walls of brass and gold fittings, doorknobs and hooks. Here you could match most accessories from yesteryear.

Tayla had spent a fascinating morning browsing before she began her article. But today she barely gave the items on display more than a cursory glance. Now that she was actually here her nerves churned and twirled triple-time.

She walked up to the information desk and, in a voice that was almost steady, she told the young receptionist who she was and that she had an appointment with Patrick McCall. The young woman smiled and excused herself. Tayla noticed her name tag read ''Leah McCall''. This was most definitely a family business.

Leah McCall picked up the phone and pushed a button. 'Meg, I have a Ms. Greer here to see Rick,' she said to whoever was on the other end of the extension.

Rick. Any slight chance that Patrick McCall and Rick McCall were two different people flew right out the window and Tayla swallowed, realising that until that moment she had been clinging hopefully to that concept.

'He'll see you now, Ms. Greer,' said the young woman with another smile. 'Just go on past the cottage and through to the other end of the building. It's the third door on the left.'

Tayla thanked her and, gripping her briefcase tightly, she headed for Rick McCall's office. Her heartbeats accelerated and she told herself not to be foolish. She was a grown woman, mature and, well, not exactly matronly now that she'd changed her outfit, she reminded herself a trifle hysterically.

There was no name on the third door but tasteful gilded lettering indicated that it was McCall's Heritage Unit.

Tayla knocked on the door and a woman's voice bade her enter. She stepped into a small outer office and behind a desk sat a petite, blond-haired woman who glanced up from her computer screen.

'Go on through, Ms. Greer,' she said with a smile. 'Rick's expecting you.'

Tayla glanced at the door in the back of the room. The wall to her left was adorned with photographs, some wonderful before and after shots of a couple of rambling old Queensland houses and she wished she had time to take a closer look at them.

The young woman looked up again from her work and Tayla made herself walk across and rap lightly on the door. As she stood waiting she felt herself grow warm in the cool air. She surreptitiously straightened her skirt, patted flat the collar of her jacket. Her mouth was dry and she felt a quickening of anticipation in the pit of her stomach.

And then the door swung open and Tayla stared in amazement at the man standing before her.

CHAPTER FOUR

ONLY the blue eyes were the same.

He wore a grey lightweight suit and a very pale blue collarless shirt open at the throat. He'd shaved and the dark stubble was gone and his hair had also been cut so that it was shortish on top, the front falling onto his forehead, and the back shaped into his collar.

'Hello, Tayla,' he said with a smile, deep creases bracketing his mouth. 'It was a welcome surprise to see your name in my appointment book. Come on in.'

He stood back and Tayla stepped into his office.

A large rosewood desk, highly polished and obviously an antique, dominated the room. But it was also evident that the desk was not simply a showpiece. A pile of files sat on one corner and a group of architect's plans he'd obviously been working on were spread out in front of what was apparently his chair.

One wall of the room was lined with filing cabinets and on the other wall was a group of photographs of colonial cottages similar to those in the outer office.

'Please. Sit down.' He indicated an ergonomic chair in front of the desk.

Tayla sank down into the soft leather, finding it exceptionally comfortable. Physically comfortable, that was. Emotionally she was still trying to regain her equilibrium after the shock of his so radically changed appearance.

If she'd thought he was attractive before, then now he was even more so. He was absolutely devastating. And

57

Tayla knew with a sinking feeling that any thoughts she'd had that she may have imagined her attraction to him died a very quick and instant death. There was no mistaking or rationalising her body's reaction to his magnetism.

What was she going to do? she asked herself desperately.

'You didn't mention on Sunday that you had an appointment with me this morning,' he was saying easily as he walked around and sat down behind his desk.

'I didn't realise it was you.' Tayla stretched the truth. 'I thought— Your uncle called you Patrick McCall. I didn't immediately catch on to the fact that Rick could be short for Patrick.'

'I guess not.' He didn't sound completely convinced but Tayla decided discretion was the better part of valour in this case and made no further comment.

Instead she unzipped her briefcase. 'I guess we should get organised. You'll be busy, what with it being your first week back at work, and I don't want to hold you up any longer than I have to.'

'No worries. As it is my first week back I'm taking it slowly.' He smiled and Tayla tried to forcibly rein in her racing pulse. 'So don't let that pile of files fool you.' He refolded his plans. 'Or this stuff, either.'

'Right.' Tayla drew out her notebook with her list of questions. Thank heavens she'd put it all down on paper because she suspected if she'd tried to gather two thoughts together just at the moment she'd have failed miserably. She cleared her throat and began.

An hour later Rick McCall sat back in his chair and glanced at his wristwatch. 'It's lunchtime. What say we take a break?'

Tayla began to close her notebook.

'I know a nice little restaurant on Milton Road. Have lunch with me, hmmm?'

Tayla blinked across at him. 'Lunch? With you?' she repeated inanely and his incredible smile again lit his face.

'Yes. Lunch. With me.'

'Oh, I don't think—' she began.

'And we can continue the interview in more salubrious surroundings.'

Tayla looked down at her notebook. 'Actually, I think I've just about got all the information I need, what with the material your uncle's already given me.'

'We both have to eat,' he said lightly.

'Well,' Tayla murmured undecidedly. How long had it been since she'd had lunch with a man? With anybody really. Mike hadn't liked eating out, preferring home cooking, so they'd rarely gone out to dine. Occasionally she'd shared a meal with a group of her fellow teachers but she'd been so busy these past few years there'd been little time, let alone the inclination.

'I promise you the food is beyond imagination. The restaurant's owned by a couple of friends of mine.'

'Well, I suppose it— But I wasn't expecting lunch,' she added quickly.

'I know you weren't. But all work and no play is no fun at all. Apart from that, my friends who run the restaurant are Bob and Jenny Ainscough.' He raised his eyebrows.

'The owners of *Meadowmont*?' Tayla said in surprise.

'One and the same. It would give me the chance to introduce you to them and set up a time for you to visit the house. What do you say? Shall we go? Combine business with pleasure?'

'Well—' Tayla vacillated over accepting his invitation. As he had said, it was business, she told herself.

She knew she needed to talk to the Ainscoughs before she could finish her article. Photographs of the magnificent historic house were available in the archives but to complete her feature, add the personal touch she knew her editor liked in her work, she would have to speak to the owners.

It was business, she reminded herself again as she nodded.

Rick picked up the telephone and pressed one of the buttons. 'Meg? Do you know if the company car's free?' He frowned. 'David took it? What's wrong with his own car? I see.' He rubbed his forehead absently. 'Well, could you call me a taxi?'

Tayla sat forward. 'I've got my car outside.'

'Hold on, Meg.'

'I don't mind driving if you don't mind being driven,' she added quickly and he shook his head.

'Not at all. And I guess calling a cab at this time of day would mean something of a wait. Sure you don't mind?'

A new tension had gripped her, one that said spending more time with this attractive man was only asking for trouble. 'No, of course not.' She held up her keys and got to her feet, making herself smile easily.

Rick turned back to the phone. 'Don't worry about the taxi, Meg.' He replaced the receiver and stood up, moved over to the door to swing it open before standing back for Tayla to precede him.

'I'll be at Bob and Jenny's,' he told his secretary. 'But only if it's a matter of life and death. OK?'

The young woman laughed. 'Right, Rick. See you later.' She subjected Tayla to an interested scrutiny as

Rick opened the door into the main building and put his hand lightly on Tayla's back to guide her towards the entrance.

Tayla tried to ignore the small courtesy but the faint pressure of his hand seemed to burn where he touched her, searing through the thin cotton of her jacket.

'I was supposed to take delivery of my new car today but it got held up en route between Sydney and Brisbane so I'm carless until Friday. And as you know I returned my borrowed motorcycle last weekend,' he explained as they crossed the car park.

'I'm over here,' Tayla said as she led him to her pale blue Ford. The car was getting old now but it still ran well. Tayla had it serviced regularly and it was reliable.

'Do you mind if I remove my jacket?' he asked and Tayla shook her head.

'No, of course not. It's a real scorcher today.'

'And coming out of the air-conditioned building makes it worse.'

He began to shrug off his suit coat and Tayla looked away, busying herself with putting her briefcase onto the back seat. Somehow watching him remove his jacket was far too personal, too intimate.

She almost laughed at herself. Too intimate? Hadn't she sat with him in Nan's kitchen in the early hours of the morning with the two of them barely clothed, she in her nightshirt and he bare-chested? Feeling all hot and bothered over his removal of his suit coat was ludicrous, she told herself before sliding discombobulatedly behind the steering wheel.

Then Rick McCall was climbing into the passenger seat beside her and suddenly the car became far too small and he was way too close to her. She swallowed as she turned on the ignition and backed the car out, turning towards the exit.

'You'll have to give me directions,' she said as he adjusted his seat belt.

His shirt-clad elbow brushed against her arm and an arrow of awareness shot down her arm to explode into a star-burst of emotion in the pit of her stomach.

'Right at the exit and then left onto Milton Road,' he said easily enough but Tayla felt a shift in the tension within the car.

Was he experiencing this same portentous awareness that she was? This acute need to run and yet to desperately want to stay.

'The restaurant's over the next hill. *The Toucan*.'

His prosaic words defused some of Tayla's nervous tension and she turned the car onto the busy thoroughfare.

'Did you say *The Toucan?*' Tayla shot a quick glance at him. It was a very well-known and exclusive eatery and Tayla knew it had consistently good reviews. 'The Ainscoughs own *The Toucan?*'

'Yes. They've had it for a couple of years. Actually, Jenny owns it and uses her maiden name. Donnelly. Bob's only been involved since he retired.'

'Oh, yes. Jenny Donnelly. That's the name. I read a very positive write-up on the restaurant in our local *Brisbane News* a couple of weeks ago.'

'That's the one. And if you turn right at the next traffic light just before the restaurant there's a car park behind the building.'

Tayla flicked on her indicator and waited for a break in the traffic. If Rick McCall could just turn up here at *The Toucan* without a reservation he must indeed be good friends with the owners. Reservations even for lunch, Tayla knew, were extremely hard to come by, especially at this time of year with Christmas approaching.

She parked the car and he was around opening her door for her before she'd had a chance to remove her seat belt.

'Thank you,' she said as she climbed from the car and turned to lock the door.

He led her across to the back entrance, knocking lightly on the kitchen door before pushing it open and leaning into the room.

'Any tasty morsels for a weary traveller?' he asked and there was a clatter of pots and pans before someone shrieked.

'Rick! You're back! Bob, it's Rick.'

The door opened wide and a petite redhead launched herself into his arms, kissing him noisily on the cheek.

'When did you get home?' the redhead was asking as a tall grey-haired man was shaking Rick's hand and slapping him on the shoulder.

'Started work this week,' Rick replied easily.

'We missed you heaps. What can we get you for lunch? I'll bet you haven't had a decent meal since you left.'

Rick laughed and moved a little and the other couple noticed Tayla for the first time.

'Oh, Rick. You've brought a guest,' Jenny Ainscough said and Rick put his hand on Tayla's back again, bringing her forward.

'Jenny. Bob. Meet Tayla Greer.'

Tayla held out her hand. She tried to ignore the speculative gleam in Jenny's bright eyes and felt herself flush.

'Tayla's writing articles on historic houses and she's interested in *Meadowmont*,' he said without preamble.

'You are?' Bob Ainscough struck his forehead with his palm. 'Yes, of course, you are. I've been reading your pieces in the weekend paper. *Dunsmara* next week, isn't it?'

'That's right,' Tayla told him.

'She's been leaving messages for you, haven't you, Tayla?' Rick continued and Tayla's colour deepened again.

'Well, yes. But I realise you must be busy, what with the restaurant.'

'You've been leaving messages on the machine?' Jenny frowned and turned to her husband. 'I knew that thing wasn't working properly, Bob. We haven't had any messages for weeks. I'm sorry, Tayla. You must have thought we were very rude.'

'Oh, no. I thought perhaps you might be away on holidays.'

'No.' Bob laughed. 'Rick's the only lucky tripper.'

'You must give us your number before you leave,' Jenny insisted. 'Now, come on through and I'll find you a table.'

'Nice meeting you, Tayla, and good to have you back, Rick,' Bob said as he disappeared back into the kitchen.

Tayla and Rick followed Jenny out into the restaurant proper and she showed them to a table for two by the window.

'I was going to recommend the grilled barramundi,' she laughed as they sat down. 'But I guess you've had your fill of that up north, Rick.'

'I have a suspicion they send it all down here. I'll have the 'barra. How about you, Tayla?'

'Fish will be fine,' she said quickly, wondering how she was going to swallow food.

'How about some wine?' Rick asked and she shook her head.

'No, thanks. Wine makes me sleepy in the middle of the day.'

'Me, too,' agreed Jenny. 'Makes me want to find a tall coconut palm and stretch out beneath it.'

Tayla smiled. She also suspected she wouldn't need any wine to make her light-headed. Rick McCall's presence seemed to be making her heady enough.

'How about some iced water?' Jenny was saying. 'Or we have fruit juice or soft drink.'

'Iced water would be wonderful,' Tayla decided.

'Make that two,' Rick said easily.

Jenny motioned to a young waitress who appeared with two tall glasses and a pitcher of lemon-scented iced water. She filled their glasses and Jenny set off for the kitchen.

Tayla took a welcome sip of her water and looked around her. The restaurant was tastefully decorated and a striped awning outside over the footpath shielded the dining room from much of the sun's glare. The gentle hum of voices and the clink of cutlery on plates was dulled by soft, unobtrusive music.

She turned back to find Rick's blue eyes on her.

CHAPTER FIVE

'HAVE you known Bob and Jenny long?' Tayla asked, completely disconcerted by his steady scrutiny.

Rick took a slow sip of his water. 'A few years. Since they took on their first renovation. *Meadowmont* is their third.' He gave a quick smile. 'And their last, according to Jenny.'

'One question we didn't get around to was, what started your interest in restoration?'

Rick set his water back on the table. 'I can't remember when I wasn't interested in old buildings. Perhaps it was my grandparents' old home. I loved it there, the absolute ambience of things past.' He shrugged. 'And I suppose hanging around McCall's since I could walk was part of it, too. I've always loved the feel, the texture of old timber.'

'I do, too,' Tayla agreed. 'I think I must have been a carpenter in a past life. I know I used to drive my grandfather insane when he was trying to do any woodwork.'

Rick laughed softly. 'I was the same. I've been doing carpentry of some sort since I was a kid. If I'd had my way carpentry would have been my chosen career back then.'

'Why didn't you? Become a builder, I mean?'

He grimaced. 'My parents wanted me to go to university so I did a business course. Actually, I see now it was the right choice but at the time I rebelled. I still make use of my carpentry skills when I can though. I'm part way through restoring an old house myself.'

Tayla raised her eyebrows.

'When my maternal grandmother decided her house was too big for her I offered to buy it from her. I'm taking it back to its original state, with all modern conveniences, of course.'

'Where is your house?' Tayla asked before she could prevent herself. She flushed a little when it occurred to her that he might think she was prying. 'I'm doing another series on historic homes after this one, on the more modest old colonials.'

'Mine is a larger than average version of the worker's cottage. It's in Paddo. Given Terrace.'

Tayla sat up in her chair. They were almost neighbours. 'There are some wonderful old homes in that street.'

He nodded. 'My grandparents bought the house when they were married and my mother was born there. The house was actually built around 1890 and it still has a lot of the features of the period.'

It sounded as though his house was a prime example of what she was looking for for her next series of articles. But should she ask him if she could use it? It would mean she would have to spend more time with him. Dare she do that?

He was Rachel's boyfriend, she reminded herself, and as such she would have to socialise with him a certain amount anyway. And as far as his house was concerned, it was business, she repeated to herself again.

At that moment Jenny appeared with their meals and Tayla admired the beautifully presented dishes of North Queensland barramundi and crisp salad. The other woman chatted for a moment and then was called back into the kitchen.

Tayla tasted her fish and murmured appreciatively. It was delicious and they ate in silence for a few minutes.

'Perhaps you wouldn't mind if I included your house in my second series?' Tayla asked him tentatively, coming to a decision she hoped she wouldn't regret.

He frowned slightly. 'The renovations aren't completely finished yet. Would that matter?'

'Not at all. It would add authenticity to the article. Apart from that I'm going to focus mainly on the history of the houses and the way they've changed over the past fifty or so years.'

'Sure.' He had another sip of water. 'I read your previous pieces this morning. My uncle had them in our archives. You write well.'

'Thank you.' Tayla felt inordinately pleased with his compliment.

'You brought each house to life somehow. You have a lot of talent.'

Tayla flushed. 'Thanks again. I guess all writers like to hear that sort of commendation about their work.'

'It's true. I could tell you loved your subject. So what was it that piqued your interest in old architecture?'

'Much the same as you. My grandparents' house up on Mt. Tamborine. It sort of developed from there.'

They continued to discuss what was obviously a mutual interest and they were sitting back over coffee before Tayla realised she'd relaxed and was enjoying being in his company, more than she had enjoyed anything in ages.

She glanced across at him through her lashes and that same heat warmed from the pit of her stomach. How she wished— She quickly put a stop to any thoughts in that direction. He was totally out of bounds, she reminded herself again.

But how she wished he wasn't.

Tayla drained her coffee cup and made herself smile. 'That was a wonderful meal. Thank you so much.' She glanced at her wristwatch. 'I suppose you should be getting back to work. And so should I. Carey will be wondering where I am.'

That her daughter probably hadn't missed her was more likely. Carey had been about to log on to the Internet to talk to Nan when Tayla left so Tayla was more than sure she would still be there. Still, Tayla had a couple of other articles to finish this week and she should be home working on them.

Rick nodded regretfully. 'I guess you're right. We should get back. I've got a full afternoon planned for me.' He grinned. 'I think they missed me while I was away.'

'I don't know who *they* are but we did,' laughed Jenny as she came up behind Rick. 'We've got a barbecue organised for Sunday afternoon. Why don't you come, Rick? Three-ish?'

'I'd love to,' he said easily and Jenny turned to Tayla.

'How about you, Tayla? And we could do all the questions about *Meadowmont* either before or afterwards.'

'Oh, I wouldn't want to— I mean, it shouldn't take long to do the interview. So I could just come along after your barbecue.'

'Nonsense. We're only having a half dozen or so people over.'

'I'll have my car by then,' Rick put in. 'You can come with me.'

Tayla saw the faint start of surprise cross Jenny Ainscough's face. 'Of course,' she said quickly. 'It's all settled then.' She planted a quick kiss on Rick's cheek.

'It really is good to see you looking so great, love. Now, I'm off down the road to replenish the bread supply. For some inexplicable reason we're about to run out. I'll see you both on Sunday.' And she was gone.

'You really don't have to bother about driving me to the Ainscoughs',' Tayla began as Rick took the bill and handed his credit card to the waitress.

'It's no bother,' he said lightly. 'And it seems like a good opportunity to talk to Bob and Jenny about their house.'

'What about Rachel?' Tayla asked and he looked across at her and just as quickly away again.

'Rachel? She'll be away doing one of her meetings this weekend, won't she?' he said lightly enough.

In all probability this was true. Rachel worked for the Queensland Fisheries Management Authority and she jetted about the state organising meetings and taking minutes. She seemed to be away more often than she was at home lately.

'She might be. I've lost track of her schedule.'

Tayla glanced across at him but before he could add any more the young waitress had returned and Rick signed the bill and stood up. After a quick farewell to Bob on the way out they were back in the car and heading towards McCall's.

Tayla pulled into the car park and suddenly remembered the photographs she needed to take.

'I almost forgot,' she said quickly before he could climb from the car. 'I'd like to take a photograph of you for the article. I took one of your uncle and Alex McCall. Your father?'

'Yes.' Rick nodded. 'Alex is my father.'

Now that Tayla thought about it Rick was very much like Alex McCall. They were both tall, attractive men who rated, and no doubt received, any number of admiring looks.

'And you want a photo of me, too?' Rick grinned broadly. 'I'm flattered.'

'Or I could simply take a shot of the replica cottage,' Tayla suggested and he laughed.

'I think I'd make better copy,' he said outrageously and Tayla found herself smiling.

'Only if you don't mind making an exhibition of yourself posing for the photograph.'

'In the aid of historical accuracy? It would be churlish of me to refuse. Do you want to take it now?'

'Might as well. And it would save me having to bother you again.' Tayla took her keys out of the ignition.

'It would be no bother,' he said, and his deep voice seemed to reach out and touch her. That same explosion of attraction burst over her again and her hand stilled on the handle of the door.

Her gaze was drawn to him and as his blue eyes met hers she felt her heart lurch painfully in her chest. Her mouth went dry and she had trouble swallowing. There was no way she could even attempt to say a word, to lighten the sudden tense oppression that clustered about them in the small confines of the car.

And then Rick was turning from her, opening the door, putting much needed space between them. Tayla pushed open her own door and propelled herself from the car. Out in the bright sunlight with the width of the car between them she could almost imagine those few intoxicating moments that had held them both motionless. Almost. If it wasn't for the continued hammering of her heartbeats.

Tayla's camera was in her briefcase and she took it from the car. The sun beat down on them as they walked across to the entrance in silence, neither of them attempting conversation.

Was he as aware of her? Tayla wondered. And the answer was just as terrifying whichever way it was resolved. Could he not be aware of it? And if he was...?

The doors opened automatically as they stepped up to them and they walked into the coolness and straight into Rachel as she was about to hurry outside. Rachel stopped dead in surprise and she threw a hasty look over her shoulder.

'Rick? Tayla?' Her startled gaze went from one to the other. 'What are you doing here?'

'I work here,' Rick replied easily. 'And at the moment so is Tayla.'

Rachel seemed to recover from her bewilderment. 'Oh. Right. Your articles. I forgot.' She glanced at her wristwatch. 'Well, I'm on my way to the airport. I have a meeting to do tonight in Longreach then I'll be back tomorrow. I just thought I'd pop in and,' she looked around her, 'and see how you were.' She gave Rick a brilliant smile and Tayla's heart sank. 'So, how are you?'

'I'm fine,' Rick said gravely and they laughed.

'I can wait inside, Rachel,' Tayla put in quickly, 'if you'd like to talk to Rick.'

Rachel shook her head. 'No time now. My plane awaits me.' She put her hand lightly on Rick's arm. 'I'll call when I get back. OK?'

'Sure,' Rick replied easily.

''Bye, Tayla.' Rachel blew a kiss in their direction and then she was gone.

Tayla glanced after her, a mixture of emotions warring inside her. Guilt that she had spent time with Rachel's boyfriend and confusion at Rachel's almost offhand manner with Rick. And why the furtiveness on Rachel's part when she saw them? And her haste to leave? Somehow Tayla didn't think it was just her hurry to catch her plane.

Had Rachel and Rick had a disagreement? Why hadn't Rachel taken the time to kiss Rick goodbye when she'd made such a huge show of affection when he'd arrived at Nan's house at the weekend? Yet their parting just now had been almost casual.

'Well, any ideas about where you want to take this photograph?' Rick was asking and Tayla drew her mind back to the task at hand.

'I thought if you stood about there and we had the cottage in the background. A bit hackneyed but it tells the story,' she added with an attempt at a light smile.

He shrugged his jacket back on and stood where she indicated. Tayla took a half dozen shots as quickly as she could, trying to divorce herself from the thought that he was almost indecently photogenic.

He obligingly moved where and when she indicated, much to the amusement of a number of passing workmates, who made wisecracks as they passed.

'Australia's Most Wanted caught up with you, Rick?'

'Don't break that expensive camera now, Rick.'

'Aren't you overdressed, Rick?' quipped one young girl with a smirk. 'I would have said you were definitely centrefold material.'

Tayla was sure he flushed slightly but he took the goading in good part.

'Lucky I had my hair cut,' he remarked dryly. 'I want my mother to recognise me.'

Having taken her photographs Tayla slipped her camera back into her briefcase. 'Thanks for that. Your uncle mentioned he'd like to see the article before it goes to

press. I should have it finished by the end of the week.
Shall I drop it in?'

'I can see it on Sunday when I collect you to go over
to the Ainscoughs'. Say three o'clock?'

'Oh. Yes. Well, I'll see you then.'

Tayla was in the car and halfway home before her
heartbeats returned to normal. And she spent the rest of
the journey berating herself for her foolishness.

Tayla slipped out of her skirt and wavered between her
navy dress shorts and a bottle-green pair. The white
blouse she had on would go with both.

'Mum?' Carey came down the hallway and into her
mother's bedroom. 'Do you think you'll be home before
me? Kirsten's father will be dropping us back at about
nine-thirty.'

Tayla frowned. 'I expect I will,' she said absently.
'The barbecue will probably finish about eightish I'd
say. The Ainscoughs run a restaurant so I shouldn't
imagine they'd want to have a late night. They must
work long hours.'

'Not everyone's an eight-hours-sleep-every-night person like you, Mum. But anyway, I thought you were
wearing that skirt.'

'I changed my mind. Do you think the blue or the
green shorts look best?' Tayla bit her lip.

'Either would look fine.'

Tayla glanced over at the cool printed dress hanging
on the wardrobe door. 'Or should I wear that cotton
dress?'

Carey sprawled out on her mother's bed. 'What's so
special about this barbecue?' she asked lightly enough
but Tayla felt her cheeks warm.

'Special? What makes you think it's special?'

'You're acting like a, well...' Carey grimaced. 'The way teenagers are supposed to act on a first date.'

'This isn't a date, first or otherwise,' Tayla denounced quickly and turned away to step into her navy shorts. 'I just don't want to be over or under dressed, that's all.'

'Who's going to this barbecue besides you and Rick?' Carey persisted.

'I've no idea. But I'm only going so I can interview the Ainscoughs. In fact I'd prefer it if I could just do the interview and then leave.' Tayla crossed to the duchess and began to comb her hair.

'Is Rachel going, too?' Carey asked and Tayla ensured she didn't meet Carey's gaze in the mirror.

'No. She's doing a meeting in Mt. Isa, I think,' she said carefully.

'Oh.' Carey sat up. 'So you and Rick are going together alone.'

Tayla continued to brush her hair. 'Rick offered to drive me. He kindly set up the interview for me and you know how long I've been trying to contact the Ainscoughs. So I, well, it just worked out that way.'

Carey was silent for so long Tayla turned to look at her, surprising a speculative expression on her daughter's young face. Tayla fought an almost overwhelming urge to babble into explanations. But she restrained herself, knowing too much of a protest with her daughter was almost as bad as too little.

'I guess it saves you getting out your car.' Carey paused. 'Rick's really attractive, isn't he? And he's pretty nice with it.'

'Yes, he seems to be very nice,' Tayla agreed evenly.

'I mean, most nice-looking guys are up themselves—'

'Carey, please. I don't care for that expression,' Tayla admonished and Carey rolled her eyes.

'Well, anyway, the good-looking ones are usually dead boring and only talk about themselves. But Rick's not like that.' Carey slid to her feet. 'You know, if I was Rachel I'd have married him quick-smart before he got away.'

Tayla turned back to the mirror, ostensibly checking her light makeup, trying to quell the sharp burst of ambivalent emotion that unsettled her at the thought of Rachel marrying Rick McCall.

'I mean,' Carey continued, 'Rachel says he's rich, he's fantastic-looking, got a great body and is sexy as all get-out. Numero uno on all counts.'

'That's not the attitude to have, Carey.' Tayla frowned at her daughter. 'Just because someone's rich doesn't mean, well— You don't marry someone just because they're rich,' she finished, sounding trite in her own ears.

'Oh, I don't know, Mum.' Carey grinned. 'It sure makes you happy in your misery.' Carey quoted one of Nan's dry homilies she repeated every time she spoke of Tayla's sister, Marlene, and her many marriages.

'Carey!' Tayla couldn't prevent a smile.

'You shouldn't have let me spend so much time with Nan.' Carey laughed. 'She's ruined me for life.'

Tayla was prevented from replying by the sound of the doorbell pealing and Carey raced out of the bedroom.

'Must be Rick. I'll get it,' she said enthusiastically.

Tayla was pleased her daughter had left the room and didn't see the hot colour that flooded her mother's face. She censured herself for what seemed like the hundredth time this week. She'd have to come to terms with this thing with Rick McCall, and the sooner the better.

She followed Carey down the hallway and she could hear her daughter talking. The deep-voiced reply set her nerve endings jangling and she stopped for a moment to regain her composure before continuing around the corner of the hall, picking up her briefcase from the hallstand on her way to join Carey and their visitor.

'I thought you had a sports car,' Carey was saying. 'And I thought you'd be driving Mum in a convertible or something.'

'And I didn't know your mother had a penchant for racy cars,' Rick said lightly. 'Should I have borrowed my cousin's M.G.?'

'I just thought Rachel said you drove a sports car. But I don't think Mum would know one car from another. I would, though,' Carey added quickly.

'Then I'll bring my new car around to get your seal of approval as soon as I take delivery of it.'

Rick McCall looked up as Tayla stepped out onto the small veranda and some sort of raw emotion gleamed momentarily in his eyes. However, the fleeting expression came and went so quickly Tayla wasn't sure if she'd imagined it or not. But its intensity made her pause as she walked up to them.

'Hi there! Your daughter tells me sports cars are not in your sphere of reference.' Rick smiled across at her and Tayla's heart lurched.

Her glance went automatically out to the front of the house and she raised her eyebrows. She had expected to see some sort of flamboyant automobile but instead a sedate white station wagon with the McCall's logo on the door was parked at the curb.

'I'm afraid I'm not a car buff. As long as they go when you switch them on I'm happy.' She shrugged. 'I guess one make of car looks much the same as the next to me.'

'I told you so.' Carey smirked at Rick. 'So what sort of car are you getting?'

'A Subaru Impreza WRX,' Rick told her and Carey straightened.

'You're getting a WRX?' she asked incredulously. 'I love them.'

'If it ever makes it up to Brisbane I am. There's been some trouble on the wharves in Sydney so I'm afraid we'll have to take my company car.' He looked at Tayla and she shrugged again.

'That's fine with me.'

'Will you take me for a drive in the WRX when you get it?' Carey asked excitedly.

'Carey!' Tayla admonished but Rick grinned broadly.

'Sure will.'

'Wow! Wait till I tell Brett. He'll be absolutely green with envy.'

'Brett?' Tayla turned to her daughter. 'When will you be seeing Brett?' she asked in surprise. She'd thought her daughter's budding romance with that young man was a thing of the past.

Carey shrugged. 'Tonight. At the movies. But there'll be Jen and Ross and Kirsten, too. We're going in a group.'

Tayla went to comment on this development but bit back the words, mindful of Rick's presence and not wanting to embroil him in a parent-daughter exchange. 'Well, I'll see you later then. Nine-thirty you said?'

Carey nodded.

'Enjoy the movie,' Tayla added as she walked towards the small flight of steps.

Rick moved back and as Tayla passed him her body tensed again in what now seemed to be its spontaneous reaction to this man's proximity. He made his farewells to Carey and then followed Tayla out onto the footpath, opening the passenger side door for her to climb inside.

Once he'd turned the car out on the road Tayla strove to find a light subject of conversation, one that would distract her from the nearness of Rick McCall's hard body.

'Thank you again for putting me in touch with the Ainscoughs,' she said evenly and opened her briefcase. 'Oh, and here's my completed article on McCall's. Shall I put it in the glove box for you?'

'Sure. I'm looking forward to reading it.' He made a smooth right turn. 'Dad and my uncle are very impressed with your series and tell me a lot of customers are enjoying the articles, as well.'

'Thanks. And I'm really looking forward to featuring *Meadowmont*. I have some background on the house, as in who built it, et cetera.' Tayla warmed to her subject and began to relax a little. 'It's only been owned by three families, including the Ainscoughs. A very interesting house.'

Rick nodded. 'And I suppose you heard about the so-called scandal?'

Tayla smiled. 'Oh, yes. A very romantic story if it's to be believed.'

Rick shot an amused glance at Tayla. 'You don't think the son of the owner ran off with the serving maid and lived happily ever after?'

'Perhaps. But I'm more inclined to believe the serving maid was sent away to have her child and her father and brothers took matters into their own hands with respect to the young man who did her wrong.'

'Ah, a realist, I see.' Rick laughed. 'Well, I prefer to think the young lovers eloped, changed their names, found their fortune in the southern goldfields, raised ten children and had a long and ecstatically happy life together.'

'Your guess is as good as mine.' Tayla smiled. 'The only way we'd know for sure would be if the walls of *Meadowmont* could talk.'

Rick drew to a halt outside the high, beautifully manicured hedge that ensured the privacy of the historic old home. Today the gates were open and Tayla walked beside Rick up the paved pathway to the wide front steps.

From the grandeur of its intricate wrought-iron veranda balustrades to the rectangle of similar metal lacework at the apex of its steep roof the huge old house reigned majestically over its immaculate gardens. At the very pinnacle of the roof a weathervane cock crowed proudly, indicating the light breeze was blowing lazily from the northeast.

Meadowmont was a prime example of a fine old lady nestled among flowering blossoms and cooling greenery. A large old poinciana tree spread its branches on one side while figs and mauve jacarandas and smaller shrubs clustered around the other side of the house.

Tayla took out her camera and framed a couple of shots for her records. What tales the old house could tell. She could almost hear the clink of a bridle, the clop of horses' hooves and the rumble of wheels on a stony road as the carriage pulled to a stop in front of the house. And she imagined she could see a dark-suited gentleman hand down a woman in a flowing white dress, a matching parasol shading her delicate skin. She could visualise the young man smiling and the young woman coyly averting her face.

And Rick McCall would so well fit the part of the tall gentleman. Tayla went quite cold and when Rick turned towards her she hurried past him and began to climb the stairs.

'Rick. Tayla. Come on in.' Jenny Ainscough met them at the wide French doors.

Amazing leadlights framed the entry and beautifully restored parquetry floors gleamed beneath their feet.

'Why don't I show you through the house, Tayla, and maybe Rick could join Bob outside,' Jenny suggested and Rick nodded and continued on down the hallway.

Tayla gazed up at the magnificent high, pressed metal ceilings and exclaimed at their beauty.

'This is my favourite room,' Jenny said as she led Tayla into a huge music room. 'Bob's a pretty fair pianist,' she added, indicating the grand piano that held pride of place.

As they moved through the house Jenny pointed out its various features, her conversation interspersed with subtle questions that drew Tayla out. Tayla found herself telling Jenny about her writing aspirations and how thrilled she'd been when the editor had agreed to her proposed series on historic houses.

'And of course Rick will be a wonderful source of information there, as well,' Jenny said. 'He's absolutely amazing and the leading authority on dating architecture here in Queensland. I suppose you met him while you were writing the articles?' she asked casually enough but Tayla sensed instinctively that this was no idle question.

'Actually, no,' she began carefully. 'I only met Rick recently. He's a friend of my young niece, Rachel Dean.'

'Rachel Dean.' Jenny frowned. 'I don't think I've met her. But then again Rick has been away up north for weeks.'

Tayla bit back the urge to do her share of questioning. Rick had been away for weeks? How could Rachel have been getting to know Rick when he was away? They hadn't seen Rachel for some time and her explanation to Tayla had been that she was busy at work. Yet Rachel had told Carey that she had met a young man and that it was serious. At least Carey had implied—

'Rick's one of the nicest people we know,' Jenny was saying. 'Bob and I have been hoping he'd meet someone nice and settle down. He deserves to after—' She paused and laughed. 'My tongue does run away with me sometimes. Come and see what we've done with what was originally the servants' quarters.'

Two other couples arrived as Jenny and Tayla rejoined Rick and Bob under the shady pergola at the back of the house. Tayla slipped her notebook and camera into her briefcase and set it out of the way. She had more than enough information to finish her article.

Bob made the introductions, although it was obvious everyone knew Rick. The older couple were business associates of Bob's and the other two, Sue and Dan, who Tayla guessed were in their thirties, were long-time friends of their hosts. Bob introduced Tayla as a friend of Rick's and informed everyone of her articles in the weekend paper.

'I've read those and thoroughly enjoyed them.' Dan shook Tayla's hand. 'I'm looking forward to the next one.'

They chatted about the subject for a while until the last couple joined them. Pete and Vanessa were also mutual friends and introductions were made again.

Vanessa Hargraves was a tall, slim, immaculately groomed woman who treated Tayla to more than casual scrutiny.

'Good to see you home again, Rick,' she said with a cool smile. 'And how's Meg?'

There was a split second of total silence before Rick replied with studied detachment.

'She's fine. She's working at McCall's again and seems to be enjoying it.'

'How nice.' Vanessa smiled briefly. 'I'd say that's just what she needs to keep her occupied, stop her sitting at home and brooding, poor thing. When Jenny said you were coming I thought you might have brought her along.'

Rick shook his head and Bob asked him a question about his holiday and the uncomfortable moment passed. At least Tayla sensed a discomfort in the others but Vanessa continued to chat lightly to Jenny, apparently unconcerned by the vibes around her.

The meal was delicious and in the main Tayla enjoyed herself, finding the small group relatively easy to talk to. During the evening Vanessa probed for information from Tayla but she sensed Rick was ever vigilant, diverting the conversation when he felt Vanessa overstepped the mark. A couple of times Tayla sensed a slight undercurrent but decided she was probably imagining it. After all, she scarcely knew these people, she reminded herself.

Eventually they decided to call it a night and Tayla thanked the Ainscoughs again for their hospitality and for allowing her to conduct her interview. Rick turned the car in the direction of Tayla's place.

Now that they were alone together a heavy stillness seemed to Tayla to envelop them and that same distinct aura of apprehension, of anticipation, filled the dark interior of the car.

'So you got all the information you needed?' Rick asked as they drove through the suburban streets.

'Yes. Thank you. Jenny was wonderfully helpful. *Meadowmont* is probably the best house I've seen in its class.'

'Bob and Jenny did an amazing job, that's for sure,' he agreed.

'With your help.' Tayla glanced sideways at him and saw the flash of white as he smiled.

'Ah, but they put in all the time and effort. And the money, of course. Renovating on that scale isn't inexpensive.'

'No, I can imagine it isn't. What little I've done on my house taught me that.'

They fell silent again and Tayla swallowed, grateful it wasn't far to her place.

'How long have you known Rachel?' The words were out before she realised she'd thought them and she tensed waiting for his reply.

He paused imperceptibly. 'I met her a few months ago. She came into the store to buy some new knobs for her kitchen cupboards.'

Tayla frowned. Rachel had a very modern unit and Tayla wouldn't have thought she'd have chosen any antique fittings. But before she could say any more they were turning into her street and Rick pulled the station wagon to the curb in front of Tayla's house.

He strode around to open her door for her and Tayla climbed out and crossed to the gate.

'I'll see you to your door,' he said as he followed her up the path to the short flight of steps.

Tayla fumbled for the catch on the lattice door, annoyed that Carey had forgotten to leave the veranda light on for her.

'I like the way you've kept the open veranda,' Rick commented as she swung open the lattice door. 'Most houses of this era had this section built in later.'

'Actually, this one was like that, too, when we bought it. The veranda was a sleep-out. When I— When we pulled up the carpet the original flooring was still in excellent condition.'

They were standing together in the darkness now and Tayla swallowed. The only lumination came from the streetlight outside so they were bathed in shadows. Tayla slid a glance at him but was unable to read his expression in the low light. Yet she sensed a tension in him that matched her own and she knew she had to defuse it.

'Well, Carey should be home any minute. Thanks for taking me to the Ainscoughs. I enjoyed it very much.' She was babbling but couldn't seem to stop herself. Her nerve endings were jangling like marionettes gone mad.

She went to turn to open the front door but the toe of her shoe caught on something, a nail, an uneven floorboard. She made a mental note to check it in daylight and then Rick's hand came out to steady her, as he'd done in Nan's kitchen when she'd tripped over the table leg. Her hand went out instinctively and made contact with his chest as she strove to steady herself.

And suddenly the timbre of the moment changed radically again.

Her mind registered that his hard chest was solid and warm beneath his cotton shirt, that he was just less than a head taller than she was, and that her traitorous body yearned to lean forward, feel the hard planes and angles of his body against hers.

Perhaps she did sway just slightly forward but later she couldn't remember if she had. All she knew was that his hand on her arm slid upwards to her elbow and a slight pressure propelled her against his chest.

CHAPTER SIX

SHE heard him catch his breath. Or was it her. And then his lips slowly descended to gently brush hers, broke that searing contact, touched again, so tantalisingly sensuous, so temptingly erotic that Tayla's heartbeats tumbled over themselves in her breast.

Heat suffused her entire body, and she felt her cheeks burn as his lips trailed a path of fervent kisses along her jawline to her sensitive earlobe. Her fingers curled into the soft material of his shirt and he made a low sensual sound deep in his throat.

And then they were in each other's arms, bodies pressed together, and he was kissing her deeply, shaking her composure and driving all rational thought from her mind. All that existed for her was Rick McCall and the delightful, delirious response his kisses elicited from her.

Tayla's breasts were taut against the hardness of his chest, her stomach flat against his, the electrifying sensation of his so obvious arousal throbbing against her, driving her way beyond all control.

She moved against him, shamelessly seeking to be impossibly closer, and the urgent ache in her lower stomach spread upward, making her breath catch painfully in her throat. His arms tightened, his hands moving down to cup her buttocks, lifting her against him, as spirals of unadulterated desire spun through every fibre of her being.

They clung together, each oblivious to time and place, to any thought of being observed or interrupted. His deep kisses drugged her, delighted her and the barrier of their clothing was suddenly an encumbrance.

Then a car with a noisy exhaust turned into the street and the rough, intrusive sound penetrated Tayla's state of reckless craving. Suddenly reality restored itself and she realised where she was, what she was doing. And who she was with.

The car passed by but Tayla told herself that it could easily have been Carey returning home. If her daughter had seen—

With a whimper of despair she pushed against him, stumbled backwards. He went to follow her but she held out her hand to ward him off.

'No. No, Rick. Don't.' Her voice broke and he stopped, his eyes glittering in the shadows.

'Tayla,' he appealed, his deep voice thick with desire, and she almost succumbed, went back into the exhilarating circle of his strong arms.

And how Tayla wanted to do just that. Wanted to drown in the newness of such incxplicable excitement. She wanted to forget the world. Forget everything and everyone. Forget Rachel.

'Tayla, I—'

'No, Rick. Please. We— I shouldn't—' She took a steadying breath. 'That shouldn't have happened.'

'It's been about to happen since the moment we met,' he said, his softly spoken words reaching out, enfolding her.

A torrent of pure sensual hunger far stronger than any she'd ever experienced surged so powerfully from Tayla's very depths it was almost her undoing. But she held valiantly to her composure.

'I don't know what you mean,' she said with so little conviction even she didn't believe it.

'I think you do,' he said evenly and she shook her head.

'You're mistaken.' She pressed her trembling hand agitatedly to her eyes for a moment. 'And that's just what it was. It was all a mistake. A dreadful error of judgment on my part.'

'On your part?' he queried, his tone ominously soft.

'Well, yes. I should have known better. I'm older—'

He gave a harsh laugh. 'I wondered when you'd get to that. I'm twenty-eight so you're only a couple of years older than I am.'

'I'm seven years older than you are,' Tayla said and he shrugged.

'And that has absolutely nothing to do with anything.'

'Seven years is a long time. You were still a school-boy when I was getting married.'

She felt an added tension in him.

'That's the past, Tayla,' he said flatly. 'I'm talking about here and now. You and me. We're adults—'

'I don't want to talk about this anymore, Rick. Let's just leave it that I made a mistake, that it shouldn't have happened.'

'Apart from our ages, why?'

'Why? You can ask that?' Tayla lowered her voice. 'For heaven's sake, I'm Rachel's aunt.'

He paused for one long emotion-charged moment and then it seemed to Tayla he went to say something and then changed his mind. Distractedly he ran his hand through his hair.

'Look, Tayla, Rachel and I are— Rachel's and my relationship—' He bit off an oath and then let out a breath. 'I guess you should talk to Rachel about it,' he said cryptically.

'And I think you should go, Rick. Carey will be home

any minute and I don't want her to— I don't want her involved in this.' She bit her lip. 'Goodbye, Rick.'

He stood there gazing at her and then he sighed. 'I suppose you're right. I'll say goodnight. But it's not goodbye, Tayla.'

With that he turned on his heel, took the short flight of steps in one stride and disappeared down the pathway. His car engine sprang to life and he was gone.

Tayla stood where he'd left her, her mind and body suddenly numb, until eventually she made herself cross to the door. She fumbled with the keys, her hands shaking so much she could barely find the lock.

Once inside she walked unsteadily into the lounge and sank down into a comfortable chair, her traitorous body reliving those forbidden moments when she was in Rick McCall's arms. And her body's reaction as she remembered the searing heat of his aroused body pressed against hers filled her with dismay, elated and yet appalled her to her very depths.

Her lips tingled and her nipples tightened and the tension of unfulfilled desire gnawed low in her abdomen. No one had kissed her the way Rick had kissed her. Not even Mike.

She moaned softly and rested her head in her hands. Mike had never evoked such a totally physical response in her. With Mike she was always in control. Always. But tonight— She suspected that much-prized constraint had been as close to being torn away tonight as it had ever been in her life.

What if Carey had arrived home and seen her in Rick McCall's arms? What sort of example would she have been setting her daughter? To gently encourage one code of behaviour and then be seen to be acting upon another. It was unforgivable.

She continued to remonstrate with herself and she was still sitting there in the dark when Carey's footsteps crossed the veranda and the door closed softly behind her.

Tayla pushed her tired body to her feet and she leaned across to flick on the lamp.

'Mum?' Carey said tentatively.

'Yes, it's me,' Tayla hastily reassured her daughter. 'Sorry. Did I give you a fright?'

'Just a bit of a one.' Carey stood in the doorway. 'What are you doing sitting in the dark?'

'Oh, I guess I just dozed off.' Tayla feigned a yawn, convinced she'd never be able to sleep again. 'Well, I should be getting to bed. How was the movie?'

She only half listened to Carey's glowing report and was relieved when her daughter left her to have a shower and get ready for bed.

Tayla lay in her own bed and, tired as she was, she found sleep eluding her. Her entire thoughts were consumed by the imprint of Rick's body on hers, his lips igniting her senses, and the heady recklessness that had taken hold of her, virtually overwhelmed her.

She attempted to define the almost forbidden excitement that still had her trembling inside. And somehow she wasn't quite able to explain it.

A small moan of despair broke from her and she tried desperately to clutch at reality, to recall how it had been between herself and Mike. In the beginning she was sure there must have been passion. But life settled down after the honeymoon, didn't it? You just went on with day-to-day living.

Mike hadn't been an inconsiderate lover nor had he been demanding. In fact, now that she made herself examine their marriage, their relationship, she realised with a flash of disquiet that she had initiated most of their shows of affection.

She had always kissed Mike goodbye before he left for work but if she hadn't she was sure he wouldn't even have noticed. He certainly wouldn't have sought her out himself to instigate a farewell kiss.

Mike worked hard and was often tired so their love-making had been sporadic to say the least. Tayla shifted uncomfortably in the bed as she acknowledged that more often than not she had been the one to need the closeness, the assurance, if you like, of making love.

She supposed Mike had not been a very sexual man. They certainly hadn't been very adventurous when it came to sex.

The one time Tayla had suggested they try to revitalise their lovemaking Mike had taken great offence and had been sulky and uncommunicative for weeks afterwards.

She had just finished reading a rather avant-garde best-seller that left her vaguely discontented and made her question the satisfaction they may have been getting from the sexual side of their relationship. Carey was away on a school camp and it was one of the rare times they had the house to themselves. Tayla had laughingly suggested she and Mike shower together.

His reaction had been to irritatedly tell her to grow up, that they weren't teenagers anymore. He'd taken her explanation that she'd simply wanted to revive the excitement of their lovemaking as a slight on his sexual performance. And he'd sulkily pointed out to her that she should be grateful, that most women complained about their husbands being too demanding.

Any small inkling that they might perhaps improve their physical relationship had been thoroughly nipped in the bud and Tayla had simply put it out of her mind, got on with her studies, with raising Carey. Until now she'd never consciously admitted that she would have enjoyed more excitement in that side of her marriage.

She almost moaned aloud again. One kiss and Rick McCall had her scrutinising the intimate side of her married life. It made her feel vaguely guilty, as though she was being disloyal to Mike. How could she allow this to happen?

It was her hormones, she told herself, and bit back a giggle. And hadn't Carey said at nearly thirty-five she was sexually at her peak. It was five years since Mike had died and she'd been totally celibate all that time.

Perhaps that was the problem, she derided herself. Maybe she was the archetypical frustrated widow woman. She pulled a face into the darkness and told herself that, in that case, any man would have evoked the same response.

Yet she met a reasonable number of men in her daily life. There were a couple of male teachers on the staff of the school where she taught. Most of the students in her journalism class were men whose ages ranged from early twenties to late fifties or so. And a couple of them were extremely nice-looking men, too. But none of them had elicited such a response.

A disconcerting feeling of disbelief rose from inside her, telling her that she was deluding herself, that it was Rick McCall alone who had the power to move her. And that she'd recognised it, had known he had from the moment he'd climbed from his motorcycle in front of Nan's house and looked up at her with his incredible blue eyes.

Dear God! What was she going to do?

She turned on her side and clutched the extra pillow

to her and for the first time in years she yearned for the warmth, the security of a strong body beside her, to hold her close.

For the next few days Tayla forced herself to concentrate on her writing. She finished the article on *Meadowmont* as well as completing a couple of other proposals she'd had in mind for some time.

On Friday she realised Christmas was only three weeks away and she decided to slip out early and do some shopping. Carey opted to stay home and chat with Nan on the Internet.

By the time Tayla returned she was hot and tired and looking forward to a cool drink and a few moments' relaxation. With her drink of fruit juice in her hand she walked through to Carey's room.

'I can't believe the number of people over at Indooroopilly Shopping Town. I think it's worse than last year. It took me a good twenty minutes to get a car park.'

'I can imagine,' Carey replied, her fingers flying over her keyboard. 'I reckon we should have Christmas in January, take advantage of the after-Christmas sales.'

'You have a point there. The prices are pretty outrageous and it's just about a bunfight in the shops themselves.' Tayla sat down beside her daughter and raised her eyebrows at the hieroglyphics on the computer screen. 'How's Nan?'

'She's fine. Don't know about Rachel though,' Carey said absently.

'Rachel?' Guilt clutched in the pit of Tayla's stomach.

'She just rang,' Carey said, not looking up from her intricate computer program.

For once Tayla was loath to speak to her niece, the

repercussions of having a guilty conscience, she told herself disgustedly. 'Did she say what she wanted?' she asked her daughter casually.

'She said something about the McCall's Christmas party.' Carey shrugged. 'But it did sound urgent so you'd better call her back.'

Reluctantly Tayla picked up the cordless phone that lay beside Carey's desk and dialled Rachel's number. Her niece answered immediately.

'Tayla. Thank heavens. I was about to try you again. I'm waiting for a cab to take me to the airport. Marie's sick so I have to do the meeting in Cairns for her. There's no way I can get out of it and apart from that I owe her a favour. I'll be away until Sunday.'

Tayla relaxed her grip on the phone. 'Oh. So you want me to drop over and feed the cat?'

'Well, no. Mrs. Evans next door will do that. Smudge has really taken to her and you know he only tolerates you.'

Tayla smiled slightly. Tayla and the notoriously spoiled Smudge, Rachel's ginger cat, did seem to have a personality clash. They always had had.

'No, the cat's okay,' Rachel continued. 'It's Rick. I want you to call him for me.'

Tayla's heartbeats began to trip over themselves and she turned away in case Carey looked up and saw her flushed face. 'Rick McCall?' she repeated as casually as she could.

'Of course.' Rachel sounded irritated. 'I haven't been able to contact him. Meg says he's out of the office but due back soon and I don't have time to keep trying him. Don't you have to check with him anyway about the article you're doing on the company?'

Tayla admitted she usually gave her articles to the

person she interviewed as a final check before submitting them. Yesterday she'd faxed off the one she'd done on *Meadowmont* to Bob and Jenny.

And she'd known all week she should ring Rick or at least his uncle before the feature went to press next weekend. But she'd been putting off making the call, excusing her temerity by convincing herself that either Rick or Duncan McCall would have contacted her if there'd been a problem with what she'd written.

'The article? Well, yes,' she agreed reluctantly. 'I suppose so.'

'Right. I was going with Rick to McCall's staff Christmas party on Saturday night and now that I have to fly up north I won't be able to go. Wish the party didn't have to be on this weekend but, oh, well, I have to go up to Cairns so there's no use complaining about it.'

'No, I suppose not. It's disappointing you won't get to see Rick though.' As Tayla said the words a hollowness clutched inside her.

'Oh, Rick will understand. He's not like some guys who get all agro if their plans are changed by a millimetre.' There was something in Rachel's tone, something Tayla couldn't quite identify.

'Rachel, about Rick,' she began and heard Rachel moving around the room, obviously packing.

'What about him? He's a nice guy, Tayla. And a good friend.'

'I thought perhaps—' Tayla swallowed. 'You like him a lot, don't you?' The words almost caught in Tayla's throat and all the extraneous noise on the other end of the line stopped.

'Well, yes. Kind of,' Rachel said uncertainly. 'But you don't, do you, Tayla?'

'I didn't say that, Rachel,' Tayla put in quickly.

'Well, I got those mother hen vibes.' Rachel laughed. 'You've no need to worry about Rick, Tayla. He's a honey.'

Tayla had no time to comment on that as she heard the sound of a car horn blaring over the phone.

'That's my cab now. See you next week. And tell Rick I'll talk to him when I get back. 'Bye.' And Rachel was gone.

'So what was all that about?' Carey's voice cut in on Tayla as she sat with the buzzing phone still up to her ear.

'Rachel has to go up to Cairns for a Fisheries Department meeting so she won't be able to go to a party with Rick on Saturday night. She wants me to ring him and tell him.'

Carey twisted her chair around so she was facing her mother. 'She wants you to tell him she's breaking a date?' she asked incredulously.

'Well. Yes. No.' Tayla pulled her thoughts together. 'She tried to ring him and couldn't reach him so,' Tayla shrugged slightly, 'she asked me to do it.'

'Oh.' Carey absorbed this information. 'Then I guess you'd better ring him now, Mum. Give him time to find someone else to go with.' She grinned broadly. 'And tell him I'll go with him if he's stuck for a date.'

Tayla continued to stare at the phone.

'Mum?' Carey frowned.

'Oh. I just...' She paused. 'I guess I hate being the bearer of bad news,' she improvised.

'Right.' Carey laughed and then sobered. 'You know there's something strange going on with those two.'

Tayla looked up at her daughter. 'Who?'

Carey pulled a face. 'Rick and Rachel. For all that she

was all over him at Nan's I don't think they're all that
involved. Nan doesn't think so, either.'

'She doesn't?'

'No, she doesn't.' Carey turned back to the computer.
'So you can stop worrying about Rachel and a fate worse
than death, Mum,' she added dryly. 'Rachel might like
him but she's not in love with him. And I'm pretty sure
it's mutual.'

Tayla didn't know what to say to that revelation so
she stood up and went into the small study off her bedroom to make the phone call for her niece.

She made a show of reaching for her list of business
numbers, knowing full well she knew Rick McCall's
phone number by heart. Hadn't she picked up the phone
any number of times this past week to call him only to
chicken out at the last minute?

Tayla stared at the receiver in her hand and as she
steeled herself to make her call to Rick the phone rang
stridently. She felt as though she literally left the chair
with fright. Now at least she had an excuse for her racing
pulse.

She fumbled with the handpiece, almost dropping it
in her agitation.

'Hello,' she croaked when she finally got it up to her
ear.

'Tayla? It's Rick McCall.'

'Oh. I was just going to phone you,' Tayla said, surprise making her say the first thing that entered her head.

'You were?' he repeated and Tayla realised he was
waiting for her to explain.

'Rachel asked me to call you.'

'Rachel did?' His voice seemed to Tayla to hold an
edge of wariness.

'Yes. She'd been trying to contact you.'

'I've just got back to the office.'

'It's about the Christmas party,' Tayla continued. 'Rachel's had to do a meeting up north. It was short notice. She wanted me to make her apologies because she can't go with you.'

'That's too bad. She would have enjoyed it.' He paused. 'As a matter of fact the work Christmas party was the reason I was ringing you. To ask you and Carey to come along.'

'Oh, well, I don't know,' Tayla began.

'It's an annual event for the staff and anyone else connected with McCall's. You did that great article so consider it a thank-you for the publicity you generated for the firm.'

'I don't usually go to things like that.' An inner voice jibed at her for being a total wet blanket. What was one party in the festive season? Other people partied all month up to and after Christmas and into the New Year. It wouldn't hurt her to go, she told herself, and Carey might enjoy it. 'It's on Saturday night?' she wavered.

'That's right. It's a big night. Santa Claus, gifts for the little kids, supper for the big kids.' He laughed. 'You and Carey live on my way so I'll pick you up about seven. OK?'

'You know, I think this WRX is just a figment of your imagination,' Carey stated as they walked down the pathway towards Rick's company station wagon.

'Patience. Patience,' Rick admonished. 'I have an absolute promise it arrives next week.' He held open the back passenger side door for Carey and then opened the front door for Tayla who had lagged a little behind the other two.

She had mixed feelings about attending this party and

asked herself for the umpteenth time why she'd agreed to go when he'd invited her. It wasn't as though it was a personal date or anything like that. And he had asked her to bring Carey, as well, she reminded herself, as she settled into the car.

'It's a shame Rachel couldn't go to the party,' Tayla commented evenly as they pulled away from the curb.

'Rachel has that sort of job, I guess,' Rick replied just as casually.

'But Rachel's loss is our gain,' Carey chimed in forthrightly and Tayla forced back the urge to chastise her daughter.

Rick chuckled and the low sound seemed to inveigle itself under Tayla's composure and set her hard-won constraint on very shaky ground.

Nice start to the evening! she reproached herself. Two minutes in his company and she was a mass of quivering nerve endings.

'So is good old Santa Claus coming?' Carey was asking him and he laughed again.

'Sure is. What's a Christmas party without jolly old St. Nick? Or in this case, St. Rick.'

'St. Rick? You mean you're going to dress up as Santa Claus?' Carey asked in amazement.

'My costume awaits me, I'm afraid.' He pulled a rueful face. 'My uncle used to play the part but he's not keen on doing it and, actually, I rather enjoy it. Apart from that, the kids love it. So. Ho! Ho! Ho! Merry Christmas, girls and boys!'

Carey laughed. 'Sounds great. But you'll need plenty of padding around your middle.'

The party was to be held in a huge convention centre and as they walked in with Rick both Tayla and Carey gazed about them and smiled. Just looking at the gaily decked-out auditorium drew a response of spontaneous pleasure.

The room had been wonderfully decorated and one of the biggest Christmas trees Tayla had seen graced one corner. Fairy lights blinked and baubles and tinsel twinkled over an enormous pile of gaily wrapped presents stacked under and beside the tree.

Children of all ages were being organised into various games and their parents sat or stood in groups talking and laughing. The sound of Christmas carols and songs filled the air and added to the festive season atmosphere.

'It looks wonderful,' Tayla said and Rick nodded.

'We go all out for this Christmas do every year. We have a fantastic group of people on our staff and this is one way we like to show our appreciation for their loyalty to the company.'

'And the place is air-conditioned, too,' Carey added. 'Very civilised.'

Rick gave a slight bow. 'Our aim is to please,' he said lightly enough.

Yet as he said the words his eyes met Tayla's, conveyed an added insinuative meaning to the casually spoken declaration, and she flushed.

Her heartbeats pounded a wild tattoo in her breast and a surge of heat suffused her entire body. What would it be like to have his strong hands, his hard body— A shudder passed over Tayla and she moved, gave a slight cough to disguise her body's sybaritic reaction to the forbidden direction of her runaway imagination.

At that moment two fair-haired young boys, followed by a much smaller girl, raced up to Rick and threw themselves at him. He seemed to be smothered by children. Rick hugged the two boys and then swung the little girl into his arms.

'Uncle Rick! Uncle Rick! Santa's coming!' cried the younger boy as he pulled on Rick's free hand.

The little girl wound her plump arms around Rick's neck and squeezed him tightly. He succumbed to this attention with forbearance, gently giving himself room to breathe.

'I've written to Santa and asked him for a transformer, the new series,' said the elder boy solemnly. 'And Aaron wants one, too.'

'And a bike,' piped up the younger boy, gaining a scornful look from his older brother.

'Pigs might fly,' he said disdainfully. 'Even I didn't ask for a bike.'

'Well, I did.' Aaron frowned. 'And I've been really good.'

'Huh?' exclaimed his brother derisively.

'Wick! Wick!' lisped the little girl, demanding attention. She put her dimpled hands on Rick's cheeks and turned his face so that he was looking straight into her eyes. 'Wick, Santa coming soon,' she told him, her eyes large.

Tayla guessed the little girl was about two years old and her cherubic face was framed by a mass of blond curls. She had to smile at the obvious adoration in the child's eyes for the man who held her. He seemed to have that effect on females, no matter what age, she reflected wryly, and then chastised herself for being unkind.

'Santa? He sure is coming, Sweetie.' Rick proceeded to give the little girl noisy kisses under her chin and she laughed delightedly.

Everyone nearby smiled, too.

'Not another conquest, Rick?' teased a young woman, effectively putting into words Tayla's own thoughts.

Tayla recognised the young woman as the receptionist, Leah McCall.

Just then a flustered woman Tayla realised was Meg, Rick's secretary, hurried up to them. 'Kids, please. Give Rick a moment. He's just arrived.'

Rick set the little girl down on the floor and proceeded to give Meg as enveloping a hug as he'd given the children. When he stepped back the little girl wound her arms around his leg and he struggled to keep his balance. Meg laughed and disentangled the child, holding her hand so the child stood beside her. The two boys raced off to join in a boisterous game that was going on nearby.

'It's great you could come, Meg,' Rick said sincerely and as she looked on Tayla sensed something left unsaid that passed between the two of them.

Meg gave a slight shrug. 'I wanted to bring the kids, try to keep everything as normal as possible for them,' she said softly.

Rick nodded and then moved so that he included Tayla and Carey into the conversation. 'Tayla, you've met Meg Lewis, my hardworking new secretary? Meg, this is Tayla Greer.'

Tayla nodded. 'Yes, of course.'

'Hello again,' the young woman said.

'And this is Tayla's daughter, Carey.'

Carey smiled at the other woman.

'Hi, Carey! And this is my daughter, Shaynah, who has a big crush on her uncle Rick.' Meg laughed softly as she glanced at Rick.

Tayla unconsciously suspected young Shaynah's mother may feel the same way about Rick McCall as her daughter did. Meg's expression had softened as she looked up at Rick and Tayla wondered if they may have had a past history. She forced herself to look away as something twisted in the vicinity of her heart.

'The other two terrors were my sons, Nicky and Aaron,' Meg added.

'How about I get everyone a drink?' Rick asked and raised his eyebrows questioningly at Carey.

'I'd like a Coke, please?' she said and Meg said she'd have the same.

Rick turned to Tayla and she hesitated. 'What about some wine, seeing as you're not driving?' he asked and she nodded reluctantly, wishing now that she hadn't come.

She felt unsettled, unsure of her place in this gathering and totally dismayed by her apparent consummate focus on Rick McCall. She reminded herself forcefully once again to remember he was Rachel's boyfriend and that he was far too young for the aging widow that she, Tayla, was.

'Me wine,' piped up the little girl and they all laughed.

Rick bent over and touched her nose gently. 'And some pretty coloured wine for the little lady,' he said, winking at her mother.

Meg sighed as she watched Rick weave his way through the crowd. 'Rick's wonderful with the children,' she said wistfully. 'He always has been.' She turned back to Tayla. 'He should have half a dozen of his own.'

'You've known him a long time?' Tayla asked and Meg smiled.

'Since we were about ten or so. We went to school together.' She sighed. 'It's an amazing relationship you have with school friends, isn't it?'

Tayla nodded and thought of Mike. 'I guess you share life's experiences, seeing each other daily, doing the same things for the most part. And friends from school seem to know you as no one else can.'

'Yes, you're right,' agreed Meg. 'School friends seem part of you.' She seemed to gather herself together. 'Are you still at school, Carey?' she asked and Carey chatted with her on that subject until Rick rejoined them and passed out the drinks.

Meg bent down and held the cup for her daughter to taste the pink lemonade.

'Talking about school, I see one of the girls from my class over there. Mind if I go over and chat to her, Mum?' Carey asked and Tayla shook her head, watching as her daughter crossed the hall.

'If you don't mind me saying, you don't look old enough to have such a grown-up daughter,' Meg said.

'I'll second that observation,' Rick agreed a little dryly as he relinquished the small tray he'd used for the drinks to a passing waiter. 'You must have been a child bride.'

'Not quite.' Tayla grimaced. 'I was eighteen.'

'I waited till I was twenty-two,' Meg said and a shadow of pain passed over her face.

Tayla wondered where her husband was but hesitated to ask.

Meg Lewis's young daughter began to pull on her mother's hand.

'Twee, Mummy. Twee.' She pointed at the brightly lit Christmas tree.

'OK. OK. Let's go see the tree.' Meg rolled her eyes in resignation. 'See you later.' She walked off with her daughter.

Tayla expected Rick to accompany the other woman but he stayed with Tayla and she felt herself tense as she turned back to him.

'If you want to go with Meg and the little girl—' she began to offer but Rick shook his head.

'I'll catch up with them later. Actually, I thought you might like to meet my grandmother. She shares your interest in old houses.'

'Meg, my dear. Good to see you.'

Tayla turned at the cheerful voice. An attractive elderly woman had stopped to talk to Meg Lewis and her conversation carried to Tayla and Rick.

'I've just been talking to your two boys. Seems young Aaron has asked Santa Claus for a bicycle.'

Meg laughed. 'He's been talking about that for weeks. As a matter of fact Rick and I chose them on Thursday night and he's got them hidden at his house until the big night.'

The elderly woman patted Meg's arm. 'And I can see this young lady wants to get to the Christmas tree so I'll let you go.' She continued on only to stop in front of Rick McCall.

'Rick! Are you going to give your old grandmother a hug?' she asked, her blue eyes twinkling.

Rick laughed. 'I wouldn't dare not to,' he said as she wrapped him in her arms. He extricated himself and drew Tayla forward.

'Gran, meet Tayla Greer who's writing those great articles in the weekend paper we were talking about yesterday. Tayla, my grandmother, Rose O'Donoghue.'

Tayla held out her hand and the older woman took it in a firm shake, her eyes shrewdly taking in Tayla in one all-encompassing glance.

'I've enjoyed your articles very much,' she said. 'And Rick tells me you're doing one on McCall's?'

'Yes. It should be in next weekend's issue.'

Tayla was amazed by Rick's grandmother. She was a

tall woman, slim and, Tayla decided, remarkably fit for her age, both physically and mentally. Tayla hazarded a guess there wouldn't be much this woman would miss.

For a few moments they discussed some of the houses Tayla had written about and then Rick glanced at his wristwatch. 'I guess I'd better go get ready. I'll be on, complete with whiskers, in ten minutes or so. Can I leave Tayla safely in your hands, Gran?'

'Of course, love.' She patted his cheek. 'Off you go or else your uncle Duncan will come looking for you. You know what a panic merchant he is.'

Rick chuckled and left them and Tayla tried to decide how she could let Rick's grandmother know she didn't need to be lumbered with Tayla.

'Let's go sit over there and we can continue our conversation. We'll be able to watch the proceedings from there, as well.' Rose preempted her and Tayla could only follow the spritely woman over to a couple of spare seats that afforded a view of the Christmas tree.

'So.' Rose patted Tayla's knee. 'Tell me all about yourself.'

Tayla laughed softly. 'That won't take long I'm afraid. I'm a schoolteacher and I do freelance writing part-time. And I have a teenage daughter. There you have it.'

'That's what I call a very short synopsis.' Rose O'Donoghue laughed. 'And I suppose you met my grandson when you were researching your stories.'

'Well…' Tayla paused and swallowed. 'He— I mean, Rick, is actually a friend of my niece, Rachel Dean.'

'Oh, yes. Rachel.' Rose nodded. 'I've met her. A very nice young woman.'

Tayla smiled. 'Yes, she is. She's in Cairns working tonight otherwise she'd be here.'

'Ah. That explains why Mac's spreading his favours around,' she remarked enigmatically.

Tayla raised her eyebrows but Rose O'Donoghue continued.

'And I was so pleased to see Meg here. You know Meg, too?' she asked and Tayla shook her head.

'No, not well. We just met actually.'

'Such a tragedy.'

'Tragedy?' Tayla repeated, her eyes seeking out the young woman in question as she held her daughter up so she could look at the Christmas tree decorations.

'You knew her husband was killed a few months before Christmas last year?'

'Oh, no. No, I didn't. How awful.'

Rose O'Donoghue nodded. 'It was a dark time for them all. Rick grew up with Meg and Trevor Lewis. Trevor's Meg's late husband,' she explained. 'The three of them were that close when they were teenagers we used to wonder which one of them Meg would marry, Rick or Trevor. Well, she chose Trevor. He was such a happy-go-lucky young man it's difficult to believe he's gone.'

'What happened to him?' Tayla asked before she could prevent herself.

'A nasty accident. A stroke of fate. You see, Trevor was an electrician, working on a house renovation, when the branch of a huge tree fell on him. Rick was there at the time, standing right beside him, when it happened. He narrowly missed being killed, as well.'

The elderly woman nodded at Tayla's expression of horror. 'Yes. Then Rick had to go and break the dreadful news to Meg.' She sighed. 'I was pleased when Rick said he was going off on his holiday. I was so worried about him. He took Trevor's death badly, kept saying he felt guilty he was alive and Trevor was dead.'

'It must have been difficult for them all,' Tayla said inadequately.

'Yes. It's not easy for Meg, left alone to raise three young children. But Rick's been there to help her. And she has her parents of course. It's been a sad year for us all.'

Tayla could understand that. She could remember after Mike was killed the numbness and then the thawing pain of the reality.

'But I was pleased when Rick said he was going off to North Queensland for a while,' Rose continued easily. 'He needed to get away, get things into perspective. Mind you, I worried about him riding that awful motorcycle. Dangerous things those. But anyway, he's looking much more relaxed since he came home. More like the old Rick, happier somehow, so the holiday's done him good.'

She turned to glance over at Meg Lewis. 'As a matter of fact we were all, both families, that is,' she explained. 'We all thought Rick and Meg might announce their engagement sometime soon.'

CHAPTER SEVEN

'RICK'S going to marry Meg?' Tayla asked, a jumble of emotions clutching at her. Why hadn't she suspected there was something other than friendship between Rick and his secretary? Meg Lewis was a very attractive woman. But what about Rachel? And the kiss she, Tayla, had shared with him only days ago? He had no right to—

'Well, everyone seems to think it would be a sensible solution. But I'm not convinced myself,' Rose added. 'I worry Rick might feel he has to take on Trevor's responsibilities because they were such good friends. Rick's like his grandfather, a very honourable man.'

Honourable? The word taunted Tayla and she felt her mouth tighten.

At that moment the timbre of the festive sounds changed. The carols came to an end and over the amplifying system came the sound of horses' hooves and tinkling bells. All talking ceased and in the hush children gazed expectantly at the door. And then in bounded a tall, portly red-suited figure, long white whiskers curled about his rosy cheeks, a bulging sack slung over one shoulder.

'Ho! Ho! Ho! Merry Christmas, girls and boys.'

Pandemonium seemed to break lose. Children screamed in delight. Parents laughed and kept wary eyes on exuberant offspring.

For the next hour or so Santa Claus passed out gifts to all the children at the party. From what Tayla could

109

deduce this seemed to be done systematically in age groups.

Rick's grandmother explained that each family gave a list of their children and the children's ages. Gifts were then purchased and wrapped.

'It's something the women in the family are in charge of,' she said with a laugh. 'And I'm sort of an honorary member of the family. My husband, Jack, worked for the company for years before he retired. Anyway, it's quite a headache getting it all organised but I wouldn't miss it for the world.'

Tayla watched as Rick spoke to each child and she couldn't help but compare him to Mike again. Her late husband would never have considered dressing up as Santa Claus, laughing and joking with children of all ages. Organising their Christmas celebrations had been left completely to Tayla.

Of course Mike had come along to the family gatherings at Nan's on Christmas Day but it had always been something of a strain for Tayla. She sensed Mike's disinterest, his urge to have the day over so he could make his escape. By the time they left for home Tayla remembered being more relieved that it was over and vaguely resentful that Mike's quiet antipathy made such occasions anything but joyous.

No, Mike would never have done what Rick McCall was doing.

But Mike was older, Tayla excused and then paused. When he was killed five years ago Mike wasn't much older than Rick was now.

Tayla felt suddenly sad. Sad for Mike because he'd missed out on so much. Sad for Carey because she'd never had the sort of father Tayla knew instinctively that Rick McCall would be. And if Rick married Meg Lewis then her three children would be lucky to have Rick in their young lives.

And Tayla felt sad for herself, for what her marriage to Mike might have been. Another disturbing thought formed, too. She felt an aching loss for what Rick McCall might have meant to her if things had been different. If only—

'Mum, isn't Rick great?' Carey had rejoined her mother and Rose O'Donoghue and she had several young people with her.

Tayla introduced Rick's grandmother to her daughter.

'Remember Donna, Mum?' Carey asked. 'Donna's a friend from my school,' she added for Rose's benefit. 'And this is Jeff who's also in my class.'

Carey seemed to flush a little as she turned to the other young man who Tayla guessed was a little older than her daughter.

'And, Mum, this is Ben. Ben Howard. He's Rick's nephew,' Carey explained and Tayla smiled at the nice-looking young man as he gravely shook hands with her.

'Rick's the greatest,' Donna was beaming. 'He did this last year and my little sister couldn't stop talking about it for weeks afterwards.'

'Rick's the best,' said Ben Howard sincerely. 'He's been playing Santa Claus for a couple of years now.'

'Don't know how he stands that suit in the heat,' Carey remarked and turned back to her mother. 'Ben was telling me he spent Christmas in Canada last year and that they had a real white Christmas with snow and everything. It's hard to imagine it being cold at Christmas, isn't it? Here in Australia we think of the beach and surfing and heatwaves as part of Christmas time.'

'I saw a show on television where cars were sliding

all over the road in the ice,' said Donna. 'Yuck! That was really scary.'

For a few moments they chatted about the different weather patterns around the world, Rick's grandmother joining in.

'As soon as the gifts are all given out they're going to have dancing,' Carey told Tayla. 'Is it okay if I sit over near the band? I mean, will you be all right here without me?'

'Of course.' Tayla nodded. 'But we shouldn't stay too late.'

'We have to stay till supper, Mum,' Carey said eagerly, obviously enjoying herself. 'Ben says the food's delicious.'

Rose O'Donoghue laughed and patted Carey's arm. 'I can vouch for that. Now, you go along with the young people, dearie. I'll look after your mother for you.'

Carey grinned. 'See you later, Mum.'

Santa Claus was waving goodbye and weaving his way through the throngs of children.

'Does your daughter take after her father?' Rose asked, drawing Tayla's attention from Rick's padded figure.

'She has Mike's colouring but I think she looks a little like my sister when she was that age.' Tayla's gaze followed her daughter, watching Carey cross the floor with her friends. Carey was taller than Marlene and looked cool and attractive in her light harem pants and top. Tayla wished she'd had her daughter's easy assurance when she'd been Carey's age.

'She's a very attractive young woman,' Rose was saying and Tayla smiled.

'Thank you.'

'And is your husband here with you tonight?'

'Oh, no,' Tayla answered in surprise, suddenly real- ising socialising meant explanations. 'Mike, my hus- band, died five years ago.'

Rose's face frowned her concern. 'I'm sorry, my dear. How sad for you.'

Tayla nodded. 'It's been difficult and I worry about Carey not having a father figure.'

'Now, Grandmother Rose, you're not overdoing it, are you?'

The man who stood in front of them was of medium height, with the broadness of a rugby player. He had dark hair and eyes and smooth, clean-cut good looks.

Rose frowned slightly as she looked up at him. 'I could dance you under the table, David McCall,' she said sincerely and he laughed, his white teeth flashing in his tanned face.

'I'm sure you could,' he agreed amiably and turned his dark eyes on Tayla. 'Actually, I came over especially so you could introduce me to this ravishing creature, Rose.'

Rick's grandmother snorted. 'Be careful of this one, my dear. He seems to think he's kissed the blarney stone. Tayla Greer, meet David McCall, Rick's cousin.'

'Tayla Gr—' He seemed to be momentarily discon- certed before recovering himself. Then he took her hand, holding it a fraction longer than was necessary. 'You know my cousin?'

Tayla nodded. 'And I think I've met your father. Duncan McCall?'

'Yes. That's my father.' He hit the side of his head with his hand. 'Tayla Greer. Of course. I remember now. The newspaper articles. Dad showed them to me. Very impressive.'

His dark eyes met hers and then slid downwards over

her body, and Tayla shifted uncomfortably. She wasn't sure she liked David McCall. Rick had looked at her in the same way, she reminded herself, and then had to acknowledge that he hadn't, that Rick's scrutiny had been different somehow, not as blatant.

'So you're a writer,' David McCall continued. 'Any aspirations to write the great Australian novel?'

Tayla smiled. 'Doesn't everyone? I'll just sit down one day and dash it off.'

He nodded, the fact that Tayla was joking going right over his head. 'You know, I can't believe we've missed each other when you were interviewing my father.'

Tayla's periphery vision caught a movement behind David McCall and she felt an involuntary rush of pleasure as she realised it was Rick striding across the floor towards them.

'So you made it, Mac?' Rick's deep voice seemed to slice the air between Tayla and David McCall and Tayla told herself she was imagining the slight wariness in the tone of Rick's voice.

'Of course. Couldn't keep me away, you make such a jolly old Santa Claus.'

'And where was Santa's helper when Santa needed him?' Rick asked dryly and David threw his hands up in mock horror.

'Now, do I look like an elf?'

Tayla's amused gaze went from one McCall cousin to the other. David was a few inches shorter than Rick and he was a little stockier. Although the two men didn't look alike there was something about their features that proclaimed their familial relationship. They were undoubtedly both good-looking men but Tayla decided Rick's face reflected a far stronger character than his cousin's.

'But I was a bit disappointed I didn't get a present,' David was continuing.

'Then you mustn't have been a good boy all year,' put in Rose O'Donoghue dryly.

David laughed. 'I admit it, Rose. I most definitely haven't.' He sat down beside Tayla and she felt herself move instinctively away from him as he turned towards her. 'So. I believe you said you'd met my young cousin here,' he remarked and Tayla saw Rick's tall body stiffen.

'Yes. We've met. Rachel introduced us,' Rick said levelly. 'Tayla is Rachel's aunt.'

David McCall's expression faltered for a brief moment before he turned his beaming smile on Tayla. 'You're Rachel's aunt Tayla? I don't believe it. You're far too young.'

Tayla inclined her head at the obvious compliment. 'I assure you, Rachel's my niece.'

'When Rachel mentioned you I rather had in mind a much older woman, a schoolteacher with glasses and grey hair.'

'Worn in a bun, I suppose?' Tayla smiled easily and David laughed.

'Exactly. I must say reality is so much more interesting.' His eyes moved over her again and Tayla felt the same discomfort.

She'd forgotten how things work out here in the real world. It was a long time since she'd been in a social situation as a single woman.

In the past couple of weeks these two members of the McCall clan had reminded her of the ways of the world with their masculine regard. Yet she decided again that she hadn't reacted in quite the same way to their scrutiny. When Rick had looked at her— For some reason she couldn't meet Rick McCall's gaze in case he saw a glimmer of the heat he evoked within her displayed so vulnerably in her eyes.

She forced her attention back to Rick's cousin. 'I believe you work in the sales section?' She changed the subject and the corners of David's mouth turned down ruefully.

'That's my department.'

'We're all part of one big family business,' Rick put in dryly.

'It makes a refreshing change from the large conglomerates,' Tayla ventured.

'We've had our share of takeover bids but we've managed to weather the storm.' David smiled easily.

The band had been tuning up and at that moment it burst into full swing.

'Would you care to dance, Tayla?'

CHAPTER EIGHT

RICK raised his eyebrows inquiringly and Tayla involuntarily put her hand in his. She stood up and he gently pulled her into the circle of his arms.

'Please excuse us,' he said to his grandmother and his cousin.

David McCall's brow furrowed slightly but he graciously inclined his head. 'Seems like you got the drop on me, mate.'

Rick smiled but made no comment. 'Duncan and Joan are ballroom dancers so my uncle always ensures the music is acceptable to proper dancing, as he calls it.' Rick looked down at her. 'Can you do the quickstep?' Tayla smiled. 'Nan made sure we could all dance properly, as she also put it, so yes, I can do the quickstep.'

'Let's go then.' Rick laughed softly and the sound magnified inside Tayla almost drowning out the beat of the band.

He held her lightly, his fingers splayed warmly on her back, the other hand holding her fingers in his. Tayla felt as though she was drifting into him as they moved as one, Tayla following his expert lead.

She was so close to him she could smell the faint clean scent of his aftershave, see the pores in the skin on his chin, the dot of each closely shaved hair, the creases in his cheeks that she knew deepened when he smiled, and the fine line of lighter skin delineating the curve of his perfect mouth.

A raw physical craving gnawed in the pit of Tayla's

stomach and she felt her nipples tingle as they hardened beneath the thin cotton of her bodice. She wished she'd worn something more substantial than the light, sleeveless dress she'd chosen in deference to the heat. She swallowed quickly, hoping he wouldn't glance down, notice how her body betrayed her.

Tayla made herself look away, focus her gaze on the other dancers. Yet every ounce of her being wanted to melt against him, feel his firm contours meld with the softness of hers.

The band went into another bracket and Rick changed their step. And Tayla automatically followed him, as though they had been dancing together their whole lives.

Part of her noticed her daughter dancing with Rick's tall nephew. The two young people threw themselves into rhythmic gyrations and appeared to be talking. Although how they heard each other up close to the band Tayla couldn't imagine.

'You dance well.' His deep voice flowed over her and her gaze was drawn back to him.

'So do you,' she replied, her own voice husky.

His eyes narrowed as he looked down at her and the sound, the people, everything faded into an obscure background. They were the only two people on earth and they existed only for each other. Unknowingly they slowed their steps until they barely moved and a heavy, electric tension wove its tentacles about them.

Tayla was sure neither of them breathed. Her nerve endings tautened, sang their incitement, and her heartbeats accelerated until she wasn't sure if it was her blood she could hear pounding in her ears, or his.

And then another couple jostled into them and the spell dissipated, dropping them back to reality. The band had stopped playing and a few couples were leaving the floor before the next bracket began. Neither Rick nor Tayla moved.

She drew her eyes from his, tried to swallow, her throat so dry it was painful.

'Tayla—' he began, her name a caress on his lips.

'Come on, Rick, old son. Stop hogging the most beautiful woman in the room.' David McCall insinuated himself between them and before either Rick or Tayla could protest, Tayla was wrapped in David McCall's arms as the band struck up once more.

'One only,' Tayla thought she heard Rick say as David laughed and swung her around in a showy manoeuvre.

Tayla moved slightly so there was some space between herself and Rick's cousin. His lips quirked so she knew he was aware of her movement but he didn't try to force the issue.

David McCall danced competently but Tayla didn't feel the oneness, the connection she felt when dancing with Rick.

'You're a pleasure to dance with,' he said after a while. 'But I could tell that just watching you with Rick.'

'Thank you.' Tayla kept her voice neutral.

'So, how long have you known my cousin?'

Tayla glanced up at him and frowned slightly. 'Not all that long. Rachel, my niece, introduced us.'

He made no comment and when the band led into a faster number David released Tayla from the conventional dancing position and swung her back and forward in a creditable jive. By the time it was finished Tayla was breathless.

They were standing waiting for the band to recommence when Rick tapped his cousin on the shoulder. David pulled a face at him.

'I thought you might want to dance with Meg,' he said and a pulse jumped in Rick's cheek.

'She's taken the children home,' he replied easily enough.

'I see.' David McCall raised Tayla's hand to his lips. 'Then thank you, Tayla Greer, for a most enjoyable dance,' he said, his eyes holding hers, lids slightly lowered with practised flirtation.

He relinquished her hand to Rick and winked at Tayla before he turned away.

David McCall, Tayla decided, was very aware of his appeal and would be difficult for some women to resist.

'I'm sorry.' Rick's eyes met hers levelly as he took her hand. 'Perhaps that was rude of me. Did you want to continue dancing with Mac?'

Tayla shrugged. 'Not particularly.' But did she want to be so close to Rick again? Part of her demanded she not put herself through the torture, while that other, newly wakened and totally alien part, craved that reckless, primal excitement once more.

'Do you still want to dance or would you prefer to sit this one out, have a drink instead?'

'I have to admit I'm getting a little tired. And hot.' Tayla fanned herself with her hand. 'It's been so long since I've been dancing I think I'm out of condition. So a drink would be great.'

As they walked towards the bar at the end of the room Rick kept hold of Tayla's hand, only releasing her to pass her her drink.

'Let's go out onto the veranda.' He indicated the large French doors and held one side open for Tayla to precede him.

They stepped outside and the door swung closed behind them. Quite a few people were enjoying the cool breeze that stirred the potted ferns hanging from the rafters of the second-floor veranda. Rick crossed to the railings and Tayla gazed in wonder at the bright lights of the city skyline along the river.

'Million-dollar view,' Rick said quietly and Tayla agreed.

She seemed unable to prevent herself recalling their kiss and she dreaded and yet longed for him to kiss her again.

She took an anxious sip of her drink, grateful for its coolness on her dry throat. 'You did really well playing Santa Claus,' she said as lightly as she could considering her heartbeats were thundering away in her chest.

His teeth flashed white in the dim light. 'I enjoy it. And the kids love it. There's nothing like Christmas when you're a kid.'

Tayla's eyes remained on his face, the shadowy light glancing off its strong planes and angles, and something seemed to shift in the region of her heart. It would be so easy to fall for—

She pulled herself up before she could even finish the dangerous reflection, terrified if she even thought it she would be lost. There's no future in it, she chastised herself severely.

Good sense instructed that she drink her drink, go back inside and simply escape from his potent attraction. It was far too isolated out here, too easy to allow herself to be seduced by the heady allure of his magnetism.

Rick moved, turning to rest his hips on the railings. 'Do you have a family Christmas? I mean, do you and Carey stay in town?'

'We usually go up to Nan's but this year my brother and sister-in-law will be away so Nan decided it would be easier if she came down here to Brisbane to spend

Christmas with us. And Rachel's mother, my sister, will be staying in Europe.' Would Rick want to spend time with Rachel's family or his own? Tayla wondered. 'I suppose you have a family celebration?'

He nodded. 'My sisters, brothers-in-law and their families go over to my parents' home for Christmas dinner in the evening. But as far as an extended McCall family gathering goes, we consider this to be the combined family Christmas get-together.' He sipped his drink. 'Do you see your husband's family?' he asked lightly.

'No. Unfortunately, Mike's parents died when he was quite young. There are a couple of distant cousins but they weren't close.' Tayla sighed unconsciously. Their different attitude to family and all it meant had been a bone of contention between Tayla and her husband.

A couple walked past them, arm in arm, and Tayla looked away as the picture they presented reminded her again of those wild moments in Rick's arms. And his kisses. She glanced at him to find his gaze fixed on her face.

He made no attempt to say anything and the silence magnified, stretched between them like a thin, taut thread that at any second threatened to snap. Tayla's heartbeats pounded in her ears and she grew hot, so terribly hot.

'Don't, Rick,' she whispered brokenly and she saw the urgent throb of the pulse in his jaw.

'Don't look at you? Don't yearn to touch you?' He gave a soft, bitter laugh. 'I somehow can't help myself when you're around, Tayla.'

Tayla's mouth went dry and she swallowed painfully. 'I think—' She gulped again. 'We should go inside,' she got out and he seemed to tear his eyes from her, looked down at the frosting glass he held in his hands.

'I suppose we should,' he agreed and neither of them moved.

Tayla took another steadying breath. 'Rick, this has to stop right now. I can't— Rachel's my niece,' she finished desperately.

He sighed and looked up at her again, his eyes dark, glistening pools in the artificial light. 'I'm sorry, Tayla. You're right. Let's go inside.'

'Mum, it's Rachel,' Carey called from the living room.

It was two days later and Tayla looked up from her computer screen and slowly removed her glasses. She hadn't danced again with Rick or David at the party, but had sat with Rick's grandmother until it was time to leave. Of course, she'd seen Rick dancing once with Leah McCall, the receptionist, and a couple of other times with women Rose O'Donoghue had explained were McCall relatives. And at the end of the evening Rick had been helping to clear up the hall so she and Carey hadn't really said more to him than a token goodbye when he arranged for a taxi to take them home.

Now something tightened inside her and she told herself to relax. There was no way Rachel could know about the feelings Rick McCall evoked in Tayla or about the kiss.

Unless Rick had told her.

Tayla's mouth went dry. He wouldn't, would he? Surely not. He seemed to be an— Tayla paused. Well, his grandmother had said he was an honourable man. But under cross examination, Tayla decided, Rose O'Donoghue would not be seen as an impartial witness.

If Rick McCall was high-principled would that mean he'd not want to upset Rachel with the truth? Or would it mean he'd feel honour-bound to tell her the actual facts?

Tayla took a deep breath. Whatever way, she couldn't let it hang over her like a sword of Damocles. She'd have to tell Rachel herself, explain her abhorrent behaviour.

But what was she going to say? That she'd had a momentary lapse in judgment? That it didn't mean anything? That it was a brief loss of control in the darkness, in the heat of the moment? A delicious, so intense... Tayla groaned softly. She'd just have to assure Rachel she wasn't to worry as it would never happen again.

'Mum!' Carey's voice rose. 'Rachel's here.'

Tayla swallowed. 'I'm just finishing up. I won't be a minute.'

She saved her file, exited her program and shut the computer down. Slowly she pushed herself to her feet and walked reluctantly towards the living room.

'Tayla!' Rachel stood up and gave her aunt a hug. 'Carey was just telling me about the McCall's party. Wasn't it great Rick suggested you and Carey go along?'

'Yes.' Tayla sat down. 'It was an enjoyable evening. When did you get back?'

'Couple of hours ago.' Rachel rolled her eyes. 'And what a pain it was, too. One of those long-winded meetings so the minutes were a disaster to get right. I'm glad to be home, let me tell you.'

At that moment the phone rang and Carey snatched up the receiver. 'Oh. Hi!' she said and her face went a little pink.

Tayla raised her eyebrows questioningly.

'Just a sec.' Carey covered the mouthpiece with her hand. 'It's for me, Mum. I'll go and take it in the study so I won't disturb you and Rachel. OK?'

'All right.' Tayla watched as Carey ran down the hall and then replaced the receiver when Carey called she had the other phone.

'Well.' Rachel chuckled. 'Bet that was a young man. Is she still going out with that Brett guy?'

'No, I don't think so.' Tayla frowned. 'At least she wasn't the last I heard.'

'Good. I thought he was too old for her. You know, all intense and macho hormones.'

Tayla smiled briefly. 'I know what you mean. Carey and I had a talk about that.'

And it had ended in Carey implying her mother may be just the right age for having trouble with her own hormones. Out of the mouths of babes, Tayla reflected, torturing herself.

'She still sees Brett but that's about it, I think,' she finished and Rachel shook her head.

'It's sort of hard to believe Carey's old enough to go out on dates and everything. Makes me feel old.'

'And that makes me feel positively ancient.' Tayla smiled and then shifted in her seat, quelling the inner voice that suggested she should remember that when Rick McCall was around.

Rachel laughed. 'Ancient? Well, you sure don't look it, Tayla.'

Tayla swallowed again. 'Rachel, talking about, well, boyfriends and things. You seem to be fairly keen on Rick McCall.'

Just the act of saying his name had her nerve endings dancing to the now familiar rush of excitement and she felt herself grow warmer.

'How long have you known him?' she finished quickly.

'Oh, quite a few months.' Rachel's gaze darted about

the room and Tayla felt her anxiety rate increase three-fold.

There was definitely something her niece wasn't telling her. 'You must have missed him while he was away.'

'Away? Oh, up north, you mean? Ummm. Yes. I guess I did.'

A short silence fell and Tayla gathered her courage to ask her niece if her feelings for Rick were serious. Part of her wanted to know but the other part, the part that was fighting for the upper hand, that wanted to see him again, kiss him again, told her not to ask.

'Tayla, about Rick,' Rachel said quickly and then stopped and shrugged. 'I should have— I mean, I shouldn't have— Oh, Tayla, you know, don't you?'

Just then Carey rejoined them and flopped down in the lounge chair opposite her cousin. 'Know what?' she asked with easy candour.

'Yes, Rachel. Know what?' Tayla repeated, totally confused.

Rachel sighed. 'That Rick and I are just good friends. That Rick and I aren't dating. I should have known I couldn't pretend to you. Oh, Tayla.' Rachel drew her hand over her eyes. 'I've done something really stupid.'

Tayla's stomach tightened as a hundred unnamed fears skittered about in her mind. She fought not to let any of them actually surface. She had to keep calm, let Rachel tell her what the problem was.

'You're not pregnant, are you?' Carey put in with youthful insensitivity and Rachel gave her a quelling look.

'Of course I'm not pregnant. I'm not that stupid, Carey.'

Tayla almost gave a sigh of relief as Rachel turned back to her.

'I guess I should start at the beginning, shouldn't I? I met Rick at McCall's when I went to get some fittings for the kitchen cabinets. You see, I wanted wooden ones to match—'

'Rachel! Totally irrelevant!' Carey exclaimed and Rachel gave her another look.

'I met Rick and we started talking,' Rachel continued. 'He's a really nice guy.' She paused for a moment. 'And then Mac came along. I mean, David. David McCall. Everyone calls him Mac.'

'Rick's cousin?' Tayla said in surprise and Rachel nodded.

'Well, he seemed to like me and he asked me out and I went.' Rachel clasped her hands together on her lap. 'And I fell for him. Against my better judgment, too.' She looked up at Tayla. 'I know Rick's a really nice guy, a much nicer person than Mac really, but Mac's, well, fun.' She looked down at her hands. 'And I really love him, Tayla. And I know he loves me. He's just scared to commit.'

'Scared to commit? That's bad news,' Carey broke in. 'Ditch him, Rach, and concentrate on Rick. I know I would.'

'David—Mac does seem a little old for you, Rachel,' Tayla said carefully and Rachel frowned.

'What's age got to do with it? He's only a bit younger than you and you're not old.'

'He's a pretty boy,' Carey continued. 'Just a show pony.'

'You don't know him, Carey,' Rachel began, obviously annoyed with her young cousin, and Tayla interrupted to distract them both.

'But I can't understand why you brought Rick up to Nan's and introduced him to us as your boyfriend.'

'Yeah,' Carey agreed. 'And why did Rick go along with it?'

Rachel sighed exasperatedly. 'When I asked Mac to come up to Mt. Tamborine with me for Nan's birthday and meet my family he said he might come. I was so excited about introducing him to you all I blabbed to Nan and Carey about him coming and that you'd get to meet him.'

She shrugged sadly. 'And then Mac said he couldn't come. He said we were getting too serious, that we should cool it for a while.'

'Only a spineless wimp would do that,' Carey said disgustedly, voicing Tayla's own opinion of David McCall. 'He's a rat, Rachel.'

'He's not really, Carey,' Rachel appealed. 'He's just, well, Mac.'

'That still doesn't explain Rick's part in all this,' Tayla prompted.

'I was at Mac's office when he told me he wouldn't come with me and I was pretty upset. Rick found me behind the shelves bawling my eyes out. He'd just arrived home from his holiday. Poor Rick.' Rachel smiled faintly. 'There he was all exhausted from his trip home and then I had to weep all over him.'

Carey rolled her eyes expressively.

'I said I didn't want to look like a fool in front of my family and that I needed a guy for the weekend to come up to Mt. Tamborine with me and pretend to be my boyfriend. Well, one thing led to another and it turned out that Rick was going up the mountain to return his friend's motorcycle. We decided he could do that and then I'd give him a lift back to Brisbane. And he would be my boyfriend for a week or two. No harm done.'

Tayla swallowed, trying to rein in her sudden, sybaritic thoughts, her wayward, so erotic fantasies. She still had no right to think about Rick McCall. He may not be Rachel's boyfriend but there was still the presence of Meg Lewis.

'It seemed so easy. But I just didn't realise it would be so, well, it was awful. And I hated lying to you all.' Rachel sighed again. 'So that's how it happened. It wasn't Rick's fault. He was just helping me out because Mac let me down.'

'We knew anyway,' stated Carey nonchalantly.

'You did not. How would you know?' Rachel demanded and Carey grimaced.

'Nan and I just knew. But Mum didn't. She was too busy worrying about whether or not you were sleeping with him.'

'Carey! That's enough.' Tayla frowned at her daughter and Carey grinned broadly.

'Sorry, Mum. Just teasing.'

Rachel giggled. 'Well, you can relax, Tayla. I haven't.'

Tayla blinked, suspecting she was losing a grip on the conversation, as her mind seemed to dwell on graphic pictures of Rick McCall's hard body, the feel of his muscles beneath her hands as they'd danced together. 'Haven't—'

Carey laughed and Rachel's grin widened.

'Slept with Rick. Or Mac for that matter.' She sobered. 'You know I don't sleep around, Tayla. It's not worth taking the chance. Besides, there are other ways—' She stopped and slid a quick glance at her interested young cousin. 'I just don't, so you can stop worrying about me.'

'There you go, Mum.' Carey held out her hands, palms upwards. 'You don't have to worry about me and you don't have to worry about Rachel. The big question is do Rachel and I have to worry about *you?*'

Tayla felt colour wash her cheeks. 'What on earth do you mean, Carey?' she asked, more than a little irritated.

Carey shook her head. 'Tsk! Tsk! As if you didn't know, Mum.'

Tayla's mind began running what was by now its favourite video. She was standing in the semidarkness, clasped tightly in Rick McCall's arms and he was kissing her the way she'd only ever dreamed about being kissed... Heat rose from within her and she had to stop herself putting her hands to her burning cheeks.

'Wow! Tayla, you look guilty.' Rachel raised her eyebrows. 'What's been going on while I've been away?'

'Going on?' Tayla's tongue felt large in her suddenly dry mouth. 'I don't— Nothing.'

Carey and Rachel laughed together again.

'Sorry, Mum. Rach and I know you lead a blameless and totally boring life. So what's for lunch? I'm starving.'

Rachel had a quick lunch with them and then dashed off to restock her groceries and finish her unpacking. She'd only been gone a half hour when the doorbell pealed again.

'I'll get it, love,' Tayla said and walked back down the hallway. Her steps faltered as she saw who was standing on the other side of the security door.

He was leaning with one hand on the doorjamb, looking off to the right in the direction of the neighbour's flowering jacaranda tree, his handsome face in profile.

Tayla's first instinct was to turn and run, hide in her study and pretend she wasn't home. But of course she couldn't do that.

And then he turned his head, saw her standing there,

and his eyes met hers. Tayla forced herself to take those few steps forwards, pushed herself to reach out and unlock the screen door. She felt slightly disembodied, as though she was moving in slow motion.

'Hello, Tayla,' he said softly and she wondered if she'd ever get used to the way her body reacted to the tone of his voice, to his mouth shaping the syllables of her name.

'Rick. How are you?' she got out as she swung the door open.

He took hold of the outward-opening mesh-covered screen and stepped inside, letting the door click closed behind him.

'Is Carey home?' he asked and Tayla blinked in surprise.

That was the last thing she'd expected him to say. 'Carey? Yes, she's home. Why?'

He grinned, his eyes sparkling as they crinkled at the corners. 'Just keeping a promise. I've just collected my new car and wanted to show it to her, show you both.'

Tayla glanced past him, saw an iridescent deep blue car at the curb. All cars looked the same to her but she had to admit this one looked aesthetically pleasing and the colour was rather elegant.

Carey walked around the corner of the hallway and smiled when she saw Rick. 'I thought I heard your voice.' She noticed the car out front and her face lit up. 'Wow! You've got the WRX.'

'Come and have a look.' Rick beamed and Tayla followed the two of them out into the hot sun.

'It's beautiful,' Carey said with awe. 'Mum, isn't it beautiful? And the gold mags are excellent. Can you take us for a drive?'

Rick glanced at his watch. 'I'm afraid I can't today.

I've got an appointment in about half an hour, then I'll be in Toowoomba for the rest of the week. Can you wait until the weekend?'

'Of course.' Carey brightened. 'Brett is going to die of envy when I tell him. Promise you won't forget?'

'Carey, don't pressure Rick,' Tayla began but he shrugged.

'I won't forget. It's a date.' His eyes met and held Tayla's, making her feel breathless and disoriented.

This man was positively lethal, she warned herself for the hundredth time.

'I'm going up to the Downs to consult on a couple of wonderful houses in Toowoomba,' Rick was saying to her. '*Crestmead* and *Mindalen*. Have you heard of them?'

Tayla nodded. 'Yes. They're both heritage listed, aren't they?'

'Mmmm. Pity you can't come with me but I'll be there two or three days.' He paused and the air between them seemed to intensify in the heat, almost crackling with a profusion of electrical charges. 'You could have used them in your series of articles.'

'Yes.' Tayla's mouth was dry and a short silence fell between them. She slid a glance at Carey to catch a slight frown on her face as her daughter's eyes went from Rick to her mother.

Then Rick seemed to gather himself together. 'Well, I'd better be getting back.'

'Have you just picked up the car?' Carey asked and he ran his hand over the shining blue Duco.

'Not a bad way to spend my lunchbreak.' He laughed and walked around to open the driver's side door.

'If you'd been a little earlier you could have shown

Rachel, too,' Carey said and he paused in the act of climbing into the car.

'Rachel was here?' His gaze flicked to Tayla.

'Yep.' Carey struck a pose. 'And she confessed to your little secret.'

'She did?' He stood up and leaned on the car. 'Ah. I'm glad she did.' He glanced across at Tayla. 'We must have both been crazy to imagine we could fool everyone.' He grimaced. 'It must have seemed like a good idea at the time.'

'Oh, you didn't fool Nan and me,' Carey laughed. 'But Mum fell for it hook, line, and sinker.'

Rick's gaze held Tayla's again. 'I'm sorry. I wanted to explain.' He paused. 'But I thought Rachel should be the one to choose the time to tell you.'

She shrugged. 'It's all right. Rachel told us how it happened.'

He went to say something, glanced quickly at Carey, and reached into the car for his sunglasses. 'Well, I'll see you at the weekend.'

Carey waved as he drove away, the car growling throatily. Then she followed her mother into the house.

'I'd better get back to my article.' Tayla infused her voice with casual evenness but avoided meeting her daughter's eyes.

Carey didn't comment and Tayla continued on into her study. She sat down and switched on the computer, waiting for it to boot up. Absently she watched the screen flash up the computer's credentials as she tried to tell herself she hadn't been pleased to see him.

And she certainly hadn't wanted to go up to Toowoomba with Rick McCall. If she'd felt a frisson of excitement at the thought it was simply because she'd have enjoyed seeing the two heritage-listed houses he'd mentioned.

Then why was she quivering inside at the thought of the drive up the range beside the man? asked an inner voice. To try to justify the way she felt by saying the research for an article had set her nerve endings jangling was the purest example of self-delusion anyone could imagine. And she knew it. As much as she loved old buildings, this exhilaration, this elated confusion Rick McCall elicited in her was an emotion she'd never experienced before.

'Mum?' Carey's voice behind her made Tayla start. 'Sorry. It's hot and I just thought you might like some lemonade.' Carey set the frosty glass on the desk beside her mother.

'Oh. Thanks, love.' Tayla took a token sip. 'That was thoughtful of you.'

Carey leaned on the filing cabinet and sipped her own drink. 'Nice car, didn't you think, Mum?'

'Yes. Very attractive.' Tayla slipped her glasses on her nose and proceeded to retrieve her file.

'So's Rick, isn't he?'

Tayla paused momentarily. 'Yes. Yes, I guess he is,' she replied carefully. Was her daughter developing a crush on Rick McCall?

'I mean, not many guys would help Rachel out the way he did.' Carey paused. 'Do you fancy Rick, Mum?' she asked and Tayla's gaze swung around to her daughter in astonishment.

'Carey, I scarcely know him.' She could feel the heat of a flush wash her cheeks and Carey shrugged.

'What's that got to do with it? You either do or you don't.'

'Carey—'

'So, do you or don't you?' she persisted.

'I—' Tayla pulled herself together and took off her glasses again. 'I think he's quite attractive and he seems like a nice person.'

For long moments Carey continued to gaze solemnly at Tayla.

'Well, he's lusting after you,' she stated blithely.

CHAPTER NINE

'LUSTING? Carey, that's ridiculous. He's years younger than I am.'

Carey frowned. 'I know that, Mum. But does it really matter? I mean, I know Aunt Marlene has her toy boys but this is different somehow.'

'I fail to see how,' Tayla said and realised her voice held a touch of wistfulness.

'Mum, there's something between you and Rick. I knew there was from the moment we met him.'

'You're imagining things.' Tayla turned back to the computer screen.

'No, I'm not,' Carey persisted. 'I'm your daughter. I know these things.'

'That should be my line, shouldn't it? I'm your mother and I'm saying you're imagining it.'

Carey was silent and Tayla glanced back at her daughter. Carey regarded her levelly.

'I just want to say, Mum, that it's OK with me. I mean, I like him and if you do, too, then I don't mind.'

Tayla felt tears gather behind her eyes and she bit her lip. 'Carey, thanks. But it's not that simple.'

'It's not that complicated, either.' Carey shrugged expressively. 'The point is, if you do like him, well, go for it. Him. Whatever.'

'Carey,' Tayla appealed.

'Okay.' Carey grinned. 'That may not have been the best way of putting it.' She sobered. 'I loved Dad but he was— He wasn't very happy, was he? I don't mean with us exactly.' She frowned. 'I don't think he was happy with himself. And I'd just like to see you get some enjoyment out of life.'

'I do enjoy my life,' Tayla put in. And she had. She hadn't known there was anything missing. Until she met Rick McCall.

'Yeah. Right. Look, Mum, you're not old. Good grief! How I've suffered over the years because of that. I mean, everyone else's mother had grey hair and spreading hips while my mother looked like my big sister.'

'With spreading hips,' Tayla added wryly and Carey gave a quick grin and appealed to whoever.

'I just don't want you to be lonely, Mum. Not over a few years' age gap.'

Tayla stood up, put her arms around her daughter and hugged her. 'Thank you, love. I know you care about me but I'm all right. I promise.'

'Just promise me you'll give Rick a chance. OK?' Carey asked seriously and Tayla shook her head in mock exasperation.

'Come on, matchmaker. Let's forget about all this heavy stuff. Let's go out.'

'Out where?' Carey asked dubiously.

'We could try for a car park at Indooroopilly, do some shopping, have dinner, see a movie. What do you say?'

Carey laughed. 'Can I choose the movie?'

Tayla pretended to give the idea considerable thought. 'Okay, but nothing too gruesome.'

By the weekend Tayla was as nervous as a kitten. Would Rick call in or not? She felt like a teenager on her first date. And it was a distinctly uncomfortable feeling.

To add to her disquiet young Ben Howard, Rick's nephew, had phoned Tayla to ask her for permission to take Carey to the movies that evening. Since the McCall's Christmas party Ben had telephoned Carey a couple of times and Tayla suspected her daughter was more than a little keen on the young man.

Ben was going to take Carey to the early movie session as he was borrowing his mother's car and had to return it before nine o'clock. Tayla sighed. She was ambivalent about her decision to allow Carey to go. Her daughter wasn't quite seventeen while Ben was a year older.

Was she being too indulgent allowing Carey to go out with Ben? Or was she being overprotective? Did every mother of a teenage daughter feel this way?

After a light lunch Tayla found herself pottering around the house beginning one job, leaving it half completed to begin another. Angrily she made herself tackle cleaning out her closet.

She soon had a pile of discarded outfits on the bed, all ready for the Lifeline bag. She stood back and surveyed her room, the huge old king-sized bed with its ornate headboard, her matching duchess, and the large old rosewood wardrobe that had belonged to Nan's mother.

For months she'd been going to move the wardrobe over to the other side of the room. If she lifted one end Carey could slip the mat underneath the cupboard and they could slide it over the polished floor. It would only take them five minutes.

'Carey! Can you help me move this wardrobe?' Tayla walked down the hallway as the doorbell chimed. Carey sprang out of her room and was opening the door to Rick McCall before Tayla could catch her breath.

He looked across at Tayla as she joined them and when he smiled she knew she was way past any advice she could give herself on being cautious. Her reaction told her she was in serious trouble, in grave danger of falling in love.

In love? She chastised herself for her fancifulness. She wasn't a gangling teenager. She was an adult and should be acting like one. Be cool. Reserved. In command. She could do that, couldn't she?

She almost laughed. Her remonstrances drifted away like leaves on a winter westerly.

Today Rick wore a pair of tailored denim shorts and a loose pale blue cotton T-shirt that accentuated the blue of his eyes. The soft material moulded his broad shoulders, hugged his hard, flat midriff. He'd obviously just showered for his hair was still slightly damp and he looked and smelled clean and fresh.

'Let's go, Mum,' Carey said excitedly. 'Rick's going to show us the car.'

Tayla reluctantly collected her wallet and house keys and followed Rick and Carey down the path to the car. She buckled herself into the back seat and admitted there was a surprising expanse of room in the interior, much more than she would have thought looking at the outside.

Rick handled the car well and Carey exclaimed on the vehicle's performance as they drove up to the top of Mt. Coot-tha.

The route, past the new botanic gardens and planetarium, was considered a scenic drive but Tayla didn't seem to notice much of the view. Her gaze kept returning to the soft dark hair that curled lightly on the curve of Rick's neck and she had an almost overwhelming urge to lean forward, put her lips against his skin, taste him.

He parked the car and they went into the restaurant

for a cup of coffee. The panorama of the city spread out below them and Carey sighed.

'Now this sure beats moving furniture, doesn't it, Mum?'

Rick glanced at Tayla and raised his eyebrows.

'I was just about to move a cupboard.' She shrugged. 'It will wait for me.' She smiled and Rick's eyes settled on the curve of her mouth.

Tayla felt her skin tingle and she had to force herself not to touch her lips. She looked away, hoping he would think she was taking in the wonderful vista of the cityscape. She sipped her coffee, very aware that Carey watched their every move.

When they'd finished their coffee Rick drove down the winding road and back home.

'Thank you for the ride,' Tayla said politely as they pulled up in front of the house and climbed out onto the footpath. 'The car's very nice,' Tayla added evenly and Carey groaned.

'Nice? Mum, this car is fantastic.'

'It is that. Well worth waiting for.' Rick grinned and turned to Tayla. 'Now, where's this cupboard you want moved?'

'Oh, there's no need for you to do it,' she said quickly. 'I can slide it over any time.'

'You may as well let him make himself useful seeing as he's here,' Carey chimed in and headed up the steps to the front door. 'And he has such strong arms,' she teased lightly, drawing Tayla's eyes to the bulge of muscles in Rick's upper arms.

'I wouldn't want to put you out or hold you up,' Tayla said hurriedly. 'You probably have lots of things to do.'

'Nothing at the moment,' he replied and held her gaze. 'And I think I can handle a cupboard.'

'It's in Mum's bedroom. And wait till you see the size of the cupboard,' Carey warned as she led the way along the hallway. She ducked into her room. 'I've got some stuff to do so I'll leave you two to the wardrobe. I'd only get in the way.'

Tayla opened her mouth and then closed it again, her cheeks pink. She didn't know that she wanted to be alone in her bedroom with Rick McCall. She wanted to demand that Carey come with them but she knew if she suggested that it would only make her daughter more suspicious. It might also appear as though she didn't trust Rick McCall. What a laugh! It was herself she couldn't trust.

A tumble of conflicting emotions churned inside Tayla as she continued on to her room. And Rick silently followed her.

Best thing to do, she decided, was get it over as quickly as possible. Tayla stepped into the large room.

'This is the wardrobe. I was going to lift this end, slip the mat under it and slide it over to that wall.'

'No worries.' Rick proceeded to lift the cupboard and Tayla manoeuvred the mat under the edge. In no time they had the wardrobe re-positioned.

'This is a beautiful piece of furniture,' Rick said, running his hand over the rosewood surface. 'You don't see workmanship like this anymore.'

'It belonged to my great-grandmother.' Tayla watched his hand caressing the timber and wished he was touching her. 'Well,' she said brightly. 'That's done. Thank you for that.'

He turned and looked at her, his eyes dark blue pools. He then looked about the room, at the large bed, the portrait of Carey as a chubby baby on the wall. 'You know, I could make myself indispensable around here,' he said lightly enough and Tayla swallowed as the tension between, tension that seemed to be continuously just under the surface, rose up to engulf them.

'And where shall I keep you in the six or seven years before I need to move another cupboard?' she asked, trying desperately to keep the conversation light.

Rick raised his eyebrows suggestively and a small smile played around the corners of his mouth. Tayla covered the flush which rose in her cheeks by turning and putting the mat back by her bed.

'Tayla. Where did you get your unusual name?' he asked softly and she looked across at him and shrugged.

'Tayla's my grandmother's maiden name. My parents just changed the spelling. "Or" to "a." It's a complicated family tradition where daughters are given their mother's maiden name as a Christian name. My mother's name was Dayle, which was Nan's mother's maiden name.'

'And Carey was your mother's maiden name.' Rick frowned. 'And Nan's married name.'

'Actually, Marlene, my older sister and Rachel's mother, should have been called Tayla as she was the firstborn daughter but at the time my father was supposedly having a feud with Nan, his mother-in-law. But by the time I arrived they were friends again so—' Tayla shrugged. 'I ended up carrying on the tradition. I told you it was complicated.'

He leaned one hip on her old-fashioned duchess and his eyes held hers. 'Well, I think I should tell you now that we'll have to break with tradition with our daughter. I mean, my grandmother's maiden name was Anderson. How could we lumber a little girl with that?'

'It doesn't run in the male line,' Tayla began and then flushed a fiery red. 'And we won't be having a daughter.'

'I can see her now.' His deep voice flowed over her, making her breathless. 'I think she'll look just like me,' he said outrageously and Tayla blinked.

'Oh. With a leather jacket and a rough-looking beard. Charming.'

Rick rubbed his newly shaven jawline. 'I told you the beard was a once-only thing. But then again,' his voice held that dangerous liquid allure, 'maybe she'll have big green eyes and rich dark auburn hair that curls just like this.' He'd stepped across to where Tayla stood and his finger touched one of Tayla's curls, let it wrap around his finger.

Tayla felt like a kangaroo caught in a car's headlights. She couldn't seem to move.

He lifted the strand of her hair, drew in its scent before releasing it, his eyes watching as it sprang back into place.

Tayla knew she had to defuse this situation before his potent attraction sapped all her resistance.

'Then I should point out that there are grey hairs in this rich auburn foliage. One arrived not long ago and now it's invited its whole family to join it. A case of misery loves company. So soon this rich auburn hair will be as grey as winter and I'll be whipping out the colour change.'

'And she'll have lips just like yours. Lips that'll drive some poor guy mad with wanting to kiss them.'

Tayla's mouth went suddenly dry and when his head came down she suspected she lifted hers towards his kiss. His arms locked around her, his lips setting her body on fire.

Dear God! She seemed to have no defence against him. His lips trailed hot caresses over her feverish skin, his hands holding her pressed to his hard length.

How could she be allowing this to happen? an inner voice asked her, but she had no answer. She should be in control. She was a mature woman, in charge of her life, raising her daughter— Carey! Her daughter was in the room along the hall. What would she think if she came in search of them, found her mother locked in a man's arms?

Tayla moaned softly and pushed against the hard wall of his chest. 'Rick! Please. Stop,' she got out through lips that still tingled for his touch. 'I— Carey—'

He looked down at her, his eyes dark slits, and she knew he was fighting his own emotions. Slowly he released her and she stepped away from him, her hand going out to that same duchess for support.

'I need to see you, Tayla,' he said thickly. 'Come out with me. To dinner. We can talk.'

Tayla shook her head. 'It won't work, Rick.'

'How do you know?' he asked softly.

'I can't. I have— I just can't.' She moved towards the doorway and he reached out, his fingers clasping her arm.

'Tayla—' The word was broken and he took a deep breath.

She looked down at his hand on her arm and he slowly released her. She led him along the hallway until they came to Carey's room. Tayla drew a steadying breath and pasted a smile on her face.

'Well, that's done.'

'Took you ages. Was it too heavy for you, Rick?' she asked, her eyes still on her computer screen.

Tayla swallowed. 'No. It was fine. Um, Rick's just going.'

'Going?' Carey swivelled around in her chair and gave Rick a level stare. 'Aren't you even going to give

him a glass of lemonade, Mum? After all that hot work?
I know I feel like some.' She raised her eyebrows at
Rick. 'It's homemade from Nan's secret recipe.'

'That would be great. How could I refuse?' he put in
quickly and Tayla decided she'd have to have a very
serious talk to her daughter.

'And I've been thinking,' Carey continued. 'I
shouldn't have left you in there with Mum, like unchaperoned. Very remiss of me.'

'Very,' Rick agreed with a grin as Tayla's face grew
hot again.

'In fact…' Carey's eyes danced with mischief. 'I think
in future you shouldn't be taking my mother into the
bedroom when I'm in the house. You're setting a bad
example.'

'My primitive, basal lust overcame me,' Rick replied
easily.

'So it sounded like. All that huffing and puffing—'

'Carey!' Tayla admonished.

'I've never huffed in a romantic interlude in my life,'
said Rick with mock indignation. 'At least if it had been
a romantic interlude I'm sure huffing would be the last
thing I'd be doing.'

'Sounded like huffing to me,' said Carey blithely.

'It was your mother. I told her to be a little more
decorous but—' He leered at Tayla. 'Must have been
my exceptional technique.'

Carey groaned. 'You know what they say about self
praise.'

'In this case I'm being modest.'

'Oh, please. Why do you men think you're so indispensable?'

'You mean we aren't?'

She smiled gleefully. 'We don't need you, you know. We can even reproduce without you now.'

'Oh, no!' Rick exclaimed in mock horror. 'Just when I thought I'd discovered the secret of the universe.'

'But don't let science deter you. We women find your animal instinct-driven urges quite amusing. So do just keep trying.'

Rick's gaze shifted, met and held Tayla's. 'Oh, I will. Be sure of that. Who am I to fight an animal instinct urge?'

Tayla drew herself together. 'Enough, you two. Any more of this sordid conversation and you can get your own lemonade.'

Rick pulled a face and followed Tayla into the kitchen. She sighed exasperatedly and pulled at the refrigerator door. It stuck and she muttered under her breath.

'We were just joking,' Rick said behind her and she forced herself not to look around at him.

'I know.' She sighed, setting the pitcher of cold lemonade on the countertop. 'I just— It made me think about, well, it made me realise what Carey's missing out on. Not having a father to, well, to talk to.'

A small voice inside reminded her that Mike would never have teased Carey the way Rick had done, that Mike and Carey had never laughed together like that.

Rick reached into the dresser and took down three tall glasses. 'And you? Do you miss him, too?' he asked softly.

'Yes, of course,' she replied quickly and swallowed a pang of guilt.

'Did Carey get on well with her father?'

'Yes.' Tayla paused. 'But Mike was, well, he had a serious nature.'

Tayla reached into the freezer for the ice cube tray, clinked some into the glasses and Rick lifted the jug of lemonade. He seemed so at home in the kitchen, moving about with her, that a lump rose painfully in her throat. How she wished—

With a sigh she handed him his glass and picked up hers and Carey's. And Rick followed her back to Carey's room.

'So what are you doing?' Rick asked Carey as Tayla set down her daughter's drink.

'Creating a web page for my boss at work. I've got a part-time job at a local printing works,' she explained.

Rick pulled the other chair over to the computer. 'A web page. Can you show me how to do that?'

'That depends. How computer literate are you?'

'Middle of the road. I'm better with a hammer.'

Carey rolled her eyes. 'Better get plenty of lemonade, Mum,' she said. 'I think it's going to be a long afternoon.'

Carey spent a couple of hours explaining to Rick the intricacies of the work she was doing. Tayla simply sat back and watched them.

She tried again to analyse her feelings, decide what to do about them. For she had to acknowledge she was attracted to this man and no amount of self-denial was going to change that.

What if she did get involved with Rick McCall? Should she simply give in to her attraction to him, get her seemingly overwhelming need for him out of her system? Would she be able to handle a brief affair? For that's all he'd want, wouldn't he? An older woman was for experience not for marrying, she reminded herself harshly.

Meg Lewis was a woman his own age and far more suitable marriage material.

Rick and Carey were so engrossed in what they were doing that eventually Tayla glanced at her wristwatch and gently reminded her daughter that she was supposed to be ready when Ben arrived.

Carey gave a yelp. 'It's nearly four-thirty. Ben will be here in a minute. I have to change.' She flew out of the study and down the hall.

'Ben?' Rick raised his eyebrows as Tayla took Carey's seat and shut down the computer.

'She's going out to the movies with your nephew,' she told him and he grinned.

'She is? Well, my nephew is sure a fast worker.'

Tayla gave him an old-fashioned look and he tried to wipe the smile from his face.

'Sorry, Tayla. It's just that Ben's always been a shy kind of kid. I'm just pleased to hear he's going out, having some fun.'

Carey reappeared in a fresh pair of cotton pants and a pretty pink dress T-shirt. 'Ben said we'd get a snack after the movies so don't make any dinner for me, Mum.'

'All right. So you should be home about nine?'

Carey nodded as a tentative knock sounded on the front door.

Ben Howard did a double take when he saw his uncle follow Tayla and Carey to the door. 'Rick. Hi! What— I didn't know— I mean, how are you?' he finished desperately.

'Fine. What movie are you planning on seeing?' Rick asked easily and some of his nephew's colour abated.

'The new Harrison Ford one.' He turned to Carey. 'Are you ready to go?'

'Sure. See you, Mum. 'Bye, Rick.'

Ben mumbled his goodbyes and followed Carey out to his small sedan.

Rick stood beside Tayla as Ben and Carey drove away and he turned and looked at her, seeing the frown furrowing her brow.

'Ben's a good kid and his mother would draw and quarter him if he didn't behave like a gentleman,' he said quietly.

Tayla sighed and looked up at him. 'I know. Ben does seem like a very nice young man. It's just, well, difficult for a mother to let go.'

'My mother once told my sister that all you can do is love them and hope for the best for them,' he said softly and Tayla nodded.

'I suppose it's a little easier in that I sort of know Ben's family. I did meet your sister at the party. Ben looks very much like her.' And like Rick, Tayla acknowledged to herself.

'And I was going to repeat that he's a gentleman, just like his uncle but—' he shrugged '—I'm afraid I'm not thinking gentlemanly thoughts about you right now.'

Tayla glanced at him and then away again. 'Rick, don't.'

She felt his eyes move over her and her whole body came alive, each separate nerve ending suddenly alert.

'Tayla, I—' He ran his hand distractedly through his hair. 'Can we talk about this?'

They were still standing on the veranda and Tayla knew her neighbour across the street was in her garden, probably watching them with interest. They couldn't very well conduct the sort of conversation he had in mind out in full view and hearing of the street.

'Maybe we'd better,' she said and turned and walked inside. And she felt him follow her into the living room.

'I want to see you, get to know you,' he said as she turned to face him.

'Rick, we can't.'

'Why not? Carey said Rachel told you our supposed relationship was just a pretence. We only ever intended that it would be for a week or two. If I'd thought about the possible repercussions I'd never have considered misleading you. In fact, I still can't believe Rachel and I concocted such a ridiculous scheme.'

He paused and his gaze held hers. 'And the worst part about it was I didn't know I was going to meet the most beautiful woman I'd ever seen in my life.' He lowered his voice and the sound, the meaning of his words tugged at Tayla's heart strings.

'Rick, I'm almost thirty-five years old.'

'I've always liked older women, starting with my mother and my sisters.'

Tayla raised her eyebrows and Rick shrugged.

'OK. Bad example. Sounds Freudian and could take us off onto a huge psychological tangent. But you'll like my mother. She and my father had to represent McCall's at another work-related function last weekend otherwise you would have met her at the party, too. So. Where was I? I'll start again. I've always liked older women, starting with my first grade teacher. She was at least fifteen years older than me and she was gorgeous. And she fancied me, too. I could feel it.'

Tayla made a sceptical noise and Rick nodded.

'She used to let me sit next to her on the bus ride home.'

'After a day with a class of little terrors she rode the bus home with them, too? Was this woman mad?' Tayla tried to stop herself imagining Rick as a tousle-haired young boy.

'She lived opposite the bus stop. All very convenient really,' he was continuing.

'I still say she must have been a beggar for punishment.'

'But very attractive. And she smelled delicious.' Rick inhaled appreciatively. 'Your perfume reminds me of her,' he said softly and then sighed. 'I wouldn't care if you were sixty-four,' he said evenly and reached out, ran his fingertip along the line of her jaw. 'I'd still be attracted to you.'

Tayla's face felt warm where he'd touched her and when his finger settled on her mouth she took a step backwards.

'I find that difficult to believe,' she said, her voice almost steady.

He shrugged faintly. 'It's the truth.'

She gazed at him, desperately fighting the urge inside her to take what he was offering, no questions asked. 'I can't understand what you see in me. I'm a middle-aged widow with a teenage daughter. You're still a young man—'

'But growing older by the minute,' he put in lightly.

'You've only just met me—'

'And I want to get to know you better.'

Tayla shook her head. 'Rick, I can't— I've been away from the, well, the dating scene for too long. I don't know the rules anymore.'

'There are no rules with me. But if you feel you need them then there's nothing to prevent us making our own rules as we go along.' He'd moved closer to her again and she stepped back again, this time her legs coming up against the couch.

'We know nothing about each other—'

'Then let's talk about us. You first.'

Tayla shook her head again, unconsciously moving closer to the doorway, and he sighed.

'Well, I'll start. Let's see.' He frowned exaggeratedly. 'I'm a sensitive New Age guy.'

'You're six, nearly seven years younger than I am.'

'I'm trainable.'

'I don't want a performing seal.'

'Ah.' Rick nodded seriously but his mouth held the hint of a grin. 'You're a modern woman who's secure enough in her femininity to let me grow in my own direction. I like that.'

'Grow in—' Tayla bit off an oath. 'Grow away.'

'You sure know how to hurt a guy.' He pursed his lips. Those wonderful lips.

And Tayla let her eyelids fall. She couldn't let him see how her gaze was drawn involuntarily to that mouth, its full sensuality. She moved into the hallway now, intent on getting him out the door, on regaining her safety.

'So. What about this other thing between us?' he was asking and Tayla drew her attention back to the conversation.

'What other thing?' she asked as lightly as she could with his hard body so close to hers.

'The sex thing,' Rick replied without preamble.

A shaft of pure desire shot along Tayla's nervous system and a fireball exploded in the pit of her stomach. 'There is no sex thing,' she said forcefully.

Rick's eyes were narrowed now, his gaze sliding from her lips to the swell of her breasts and Tayla wanted to cover the rapid beating of the pulse at the base of her throat. But Rick's attention focused on it, lingered, and then slowly rose to look her in the eyes.

'Isn't there?' he asked with soft seriousness and his hand reached out, his fingertip touching her throat, settling on that erratic, so vulnerable vibration.

CHAPTER TEN

TAYLA pressed against the hallway wall, unsure whether she leant there for the support it gave or to put herself as far from the potent magnetism that was Rick McCall as possible.

'I'm not a pushover, Rick, or easy—' she began and he grinned lopsidedly.

'Definitely not easy,' he said wryly.

'And I'm not a frustrated widow—'

Rick groaned softly. 'At this moment I could almost wish you were.'

Their eyes met.

'Then perhaps you mightn't be able to stop yourself tearing my clothes off,' he added thickly. He moved closer, ran his knuckle gently down the smooth skin of her cheek and Tayla burned. His hand opened, cupped the side of her face, his fingertips lingering on her lips. 'But you're not frustrated.'

Tayla tried to turn away, break the searing contact, but she found she couldn't quite do that. When she did move it was to gently press her lips into his palm.

She felt his hand tremble and she looked up at him again. His eyes were shadowy blue and his lips had softened into a full, sensual curve.

Tayla's blood began to race in her veins and her skin grew hot, burning where his palm still cupped her face.

His molten gaze seemed to flow over each of her features, settled on her mouth, and he softly traced the outline of her lips with the pad of his thumb. The contact was velvety, barely discernible, but to Tayla it felt as though he was indelibly printing his touch upon her.

Then the movement of his thumb stopped and, with oh-so-gentle pressure his thumb slipped into her mouth. Tayla's lips pursed involuntarily around it, her teeth nibbling on his sensitised skin and she heard him draw a sharp breath.

With a low moan he leaned closer into her and his hands slid across her shoulders, lightly down the tingling skin of her bare arms, to settle on the swell of her hips. And Tayla's knees trembled, her legs threatening to give way beneath her. She was glad again of the support of the solid wall behind her.

He lowered his head, his lips tantalising the soft skin in the curve at the side of her neck.

'You feel so good,' he murmured thickly and then his lips moved upwards, his teeth nibbling on her sensitive earlobe.

Tayla's body reacted instantaneously, tensed as goose bumps swept over the surface of her body. She threw back her head and he kissed the tender skin of her throat, sought and found the pulse that beat so erratically there.

And then his lips claimed hers and she knew without a doubt she was lost. His tongue tip teased, insinuated itself to taste the inside of her mouth and Tayla clutched him to her as her muscles tightened, as taut and anticipatory as finely tuned guitar strings.

His strong hands left her hips, moved upwards to cup her breasts, and Tayla's breath caught in her throat as his palms brushed her so-aroused nipples through the thin material of her shirt. As his fingers caressed her she moaned softly deep in her throat.

For a split second she subconsciously recognised it was a tone so unlike any she'd ever uttered, yet just the sound of it seemed to inflame her even more. She melted against him, exhilarated by the heady eroticism of his hard arousal pressed urgently against her.

She wanted to throw off her clothes, and his, rid them of the frustrating barrier. She needed to feel his hot bare skin against hers, feel him surge inside her, assuaging this driving need he had unleashed within her.

He pulled her shirt from the waistband of her shorts and slipped his hands beneath the material, sliding his hands up over her bare midriff. And her skin burned. He cupped her lace-covered breasts, sending shivers of delight careering over every quivering millimetre of her body.

Tayla leaned forward, reached out with trembling hands to drag his own shirt from his shorts and she let her fingers rove over his firm flesh, the light matt of hair on his hard chest. Her hands covered each contour, found his small hard nipples, his well-defined musculature.

Her fingers moved to fumble with the buckle of his belt and he moved slightly so that his own hands could cover and still hers. Tayla looked up at him, her eyes burning with her arousal, her lips swollen and inviting, and Rick groaned.

'God! Tayla! Don't look at me like that. Not here in the open doorway.'

Her gaze slid sideways and she realised they were leaning into each other in the hallway in front of the door. The security screen was closed but any passer-by could have glanced in and seen them. And probably had.

Tayla felt her colour deepen. 'I'm— Oh, Rick,' she said on a half sob as her voice broke.

Yet her desire hadn't been lessened by the knowledge that she could behave so wantonly. She suspected if he'd made a move to take her there and then she wouldn't have been able to deny him. Or herself.

And then he was swinging her into his arms and walking down the hallway towards her room.

'Rick, put me down.' She clutched at his broad shoulders, felt the ripple of hard muscles. 'I'm too heavy. You'll hurt yourself.'

'Heaven forbid,' he said lightly and gave a low chuckle. 'Don't forget I've had a practice run earlier with the wardrobe.'

He manoeuvred them into the bedroom and then slowly let her body slide down his until her feet touched the floor.

His lips claimed hers, kissed her urgently, and Tayla responded with all the pent-up desire that surged within her.

His hands lifted her shirt over her head and Tayla dispensed with his. She leaned forward so he could reach around, unclip her bra. His fingers slipped with deliberate slowness around to insinuate themselves under the fine lace. And when his fingertips reached her nipples Tayla dissolved against him, her full breasts grazing his warm skin.

He took her naked breasts in his hands and leaned forward, thumbs gently stroking her until she thought she would be unable to bear the heightened sensations a moment longer. Then his lips captured first one rosy peak and then the other, teasing with his tongue and teeth, gently suckling. With a low moan he buried his face into them, drawing in the feel, the scent of them.

Tayla murmured, low, enraptured, completely captivated, as he continued to caress her. His hands slipped her shorts and panties downwards and she hurriedly stepped out of them and stood naked before him.

His eyes drank in her body and she knew a momentary urge to cover herself, protect her far from slender curves from his ardent gaze.

'You're beautiful,' he murmured. 'So incredibly beautiful.'

He went down on one knee, letting his lips trail downwards over the slight mound of her stomach to the triangle of deep auburn curls.

A shaft of desire arrowed through Tayla, burst in a kaleidoscope in the pit of her stomach, and she sagged against him, her fingers twined in his hair, his name trembling on her lips.

He stood up, steadied her, moved her towards the bed and threw back the covers, sending her previously discarded pile of clothing onto the floor. Then he lowered her gently back onto the bed's soft surface.

She gazed up at him with languid sensuousness and he shook his head.

'You're so incredibly beautiful, do you know that?' he asked thickly. 'I don't think I'll be able to— I want to— God! Tayla!'

He stood beside her and his hands shook as he unbuckled his belt, fumbled to lower his zip, let his denim shorts fall to the floor. Then he was slipping out of his brief black underpants.

Tayla pushed herself up onto one elbow and reached out to touch him, feel the smooth hardness of him. He made a low-pitched, impassioned moan deep in his throat and sank onto the bed, stretching his hard length beside her.

His fingers skimmed her supersensitive skin, rekindling her aching need. Her nipples hardened as he caressed them with his mouth while his hands slid downwards, seeking and instinctively finding each craving, to that so erotic place. She arched against him, her lips raining hot kisses on his chest, his chin, and finally, finding his delicious mouth.

He moved over her and she opened to him as he lowered himself onto her. Then he was inside her, surging, swelling within her.

As they moved together, Tayla's fingers danced delightedly over his back, his firm buttocks, the indentation of his backbone, luxuriating in the play of his hard muscles. Her body was so alive, heat throbbing through her, and then suddenly she grew tense, crying out as she was caught in a tumult, overcome by cascading waves of pure pleasure.

Rick's breath escaped on a shuddering release and he relaxed over her, taking his weight on his elbows until their breathing had returned to some semblance of normality. After a moment he slowly slid from her to lie beside her.

Tayla clutched him to her, all at once bereft, and he murmured soothingly, tucking her head onto his shoulder, his arms wrapped around her. They held each other for long moments.

'Rick, I—' Tayla took a steadying breath, glanced up at him. 'That was wonderful.'

The creases in his cheeks deepened as he smiled. 'I couldn't have put it better myself.'

'I meant it, Rick,' Tayla told him and he looked down at her.

'Believe me, so did I.' He leaned across and kissed her tenderly.

'I— It's never been like, well, like that for me.' She flushed and looked away from him.

He took her chin in his fingers and gently turned her face until she was looking at him. 'It was the same for

me, too,' he said with seemingly honest straightforward-
ness.

'But men—' Tayla sought the right words. 'I thought
it was— I mean, with men—'

He raised his dark brows. 'Along the lines of *Any port
in a storm?*'

'Well, yes.'

'Not this man, Tayla. Believe me, not this man.'

Her eyes searched his face, her heart desperately
wanting to trust him. Dare she? How she wanted to.

He kissed her again, slowly, almost reverently, and
Tayla sighed.

She wanted to clasp this moment to her, not allow
reality to take hold of them again, snatch the moment
away from her. But she knew she was asking for the
impossible. And she was getting far too intense.

'You're very good.' She forced a lightness into her
voice and he grinned.

'Why, thank you, ma'am. I aim to please. But I've
heard it said you're only as good as your partner, uh,
shall we say, encourages you to be.'

Tayla smiled, too. 'Then perhaps Carey was right. Not
long ago she implied that at my advanced age I was
considered to be at my sexual peak. Do you think she
may have been right?'

'Ah. That has to be the answer.' Rick chuckled. 'And
I'm doubly blessed.'

'Oh?'

'Once for being in the right place. And twice for being
there at the right time.'

'And it appears I'm also fortunate enough to have the
benefit of your exceptional technique.' Tayla ran her
hand downwards over his flat stomach and he groaned
ruefully.

'I just wish I was about fifteen or sixteen myself and in *my* prime.'

She laughed softly. 'I don't think you need to worry. In my very humble opinion you're doing fine.'

Rick's hand settled lightly over the swell of her breast and he raised himself on one elbow to bury his face in their softness again. 'Perhaps in a little while, hmm?'

Tayla felt him stir against her and Rick grinned sheepishly.

'Well. Maybe sooner. You've got me striving for greater heights.'

She moved her hand and Rick groaned again. 'Higher than before? Mmm,' she murmured thickly. 'I can't wait.'

And his lips found hers.

Afterwards they lay in each other's arms and, totally satiated, Tayla drifted off to sleep. She stirred when she felt the mattress move and opened her eyes to see Rick sitting beside her on the bed, a small tray in his hands.

'We missed dinner so I made us a sandwich. With all this activity we need sustenance, don't you think? And I found some white wine. So, let's have a picnic.'

And suddenly Tayla realised she was ravenously hungry. They sat side by side on the bed and ate the ham and salad sandwiches Rick had made. When Tayla dropped a crumb Rick leaned over and licked it from her body. They sipped the cool wine, kissed each other lingeringly, and when Tayla lay back on the bed Rick trickled wine on her breasts and slowly slurped it up, drop by drop.

Tayla felt a faint spark of renewed arousal and she glanced across at her bedside clock. 'Oh, no.' She sighed regretfully. 'We'd better get dressed. Carey and Ben will be home soon.'

Rick's tongue tip captured an errant trickle of wine and Tayla shivered.

'Are you sure we don't have time?' he asked, his eyes sparkling with his own rekindling fire.

Tayla's resolve wavered and then she reluctantly shook her head. 'No. I— Rick, I don't want to take the chance on Carey walking in on us or anything.'

He held her gaze. 'It's OK, Tayla.' He ran his hand reassuringly along her arm. 'I understand that. I can see how difficult it is raising kids these days and if you say one thing and do the other, well, you lose credibility and their respect. It's not easy, is it?'

Tayla shook her head. 'No, it's not.' She reached out and ran her hand over his slightly beard-roughened jawline. 'It's not that I don't want to.'

'I know.' He took her hand and kissed her palm. 'Come on. I'll help you make the bed.' He grinned. 'Get rid of the evidence.'

They pulled up the bedclothes and smoothed the bedspread, returning Tayla's pile of clothes to the bed, laughing like a couple of children covering up a misdemeanour. Rick picked up Tayla's panties and jokingly went to climb into them.

'Oops! Yours, I think. Mixing knickers is a dead giveaway.'

Tayla giggled. 'I prefer you in those scanty black things you were almost wearing.'

He'd donned his brief underpants and posed for her. 'These? I thought they looked very fetching. At least, I hoped you'd think so when I put them on.'

Tayla's smile faltered slightly. 'You were that sure of me?'

He rolled his eyes exasperatedly. 'Sure of you? I've never been less sure of anything in my life. No, Tayla,

I wasn't sure of you. But I can't deny I wanted this to happen. The thought of it has kept me wide awake and in need of a cold shower since the moment we met. I wanted you in my arms, wanted to make love to you.'

She held his level gaze, a myriad conflicting emotions warring inside her. Could she trust him?

'And I have to confess I bought a half dozen pairs of these.' He indicated his underpants. 'In assorted colours. I was going to keep wearing them, rotating the colours, on the off chance I'd eventually get to impress you. I wasn't going to give up.'

He paused, his blue eyes on her. 'So, were you?'

Tayla's mouth went dry. 'Was I what?' she asked, playing for time.

'Were you impressed?' he repeated softly, and although he was smiling, she thought she caught a flicker of uncertainty in his expression and it tugged at her heartstrings.

'Yes, I was impressed,' she said honestly as her eyes drank him in again.

He sighed and picked up his shorts. 'Good,' he said. 'Very good.'

They finished dressing in silence and some of the earlier tension grew between them again. Rick collected the tray of plates and glasses from their snack and followed Tayla out of the bedroom.

In the living room once more Tayla went to sit down but he took her hand, pulled her back into the circle of his arms.

'I want to see you again,' he said softly and Tayla leaned into him.

Yet her inner voice told her not to allow this situation to get out of control, demanded that she not be a fool, that she not let him get too close, that she could grow too used to having him here with her. In her life. And in her bed.

Tayla's head spun. Wouldn't he soon tire of her? Find a younger, prettier woman to try to impress? She suspected he would.

But how she wished she could believe he was genuine, that he could feel for her what she'd known all along she felt for him. She was falling, had fallen, in love with him. Wildly. Deeply. Inappropriately. So foolishly in love with him.

Footsteps sounded on the veranda and Carey's key scraped in the lock of the security screen. Tayla almost sprang out of Rick's embrace. She ran a shaking hand through her hair and agitatedly patted her shirt, checking it was in place. She gave Rick one last look before she moved into the hallway.

'Hi!' she greeted her daughter brightly as Carey came through the door, Ben hovering reticently behind her.

Carey's gaze went levelly to Rick as he joined her mother. 'I was surprised to see your car still here, Rick. Did you have dinner with Mum?'

Tayla guiltily avoided her daughter's eyes. Guilty? She admonished herself. Although she was Carey's mother she was still an adult, a single adult, so, she told herself, she had no reason to feel guilty. It wasn't as though she had done anything disreputable in front of her daughter.

'Yes, I did,' Rick was replying evenly. 'Hope you don't mind.'

Carey shook her head. 'No, of course not. Actually, it was good Mum wasn't just sitting here on her own.'

Tayla suddenly saw herself as a little old woman nodding off in her rocking chair and she suppressed a hysterical desire to laugh.

'So, how was the movie?' Rick asked the young couple, easily filling the short silence.

'Great!' Carey and Ben replied in unison.

'You'll have to go and see it,' Carey added and then turned to Ben. 'Thanks for taking me.'

The young man flushed. 'That's OK. My pleasure.' He shifted uncomfortably.

'Would you care for a drink, Ben?' Tayla asked politely and he shook his head.

'No, thanks, Mrs. Greer. Well, I guess I'd better go take Mum's car back. I— I'll see you later, Carey.' He dragged his eyes from the young girl. 'Goodnight, Mrs. Greer. See you, Rick.' He turned and loped out to his car.

Carey waved him goodbye and then followed her mother and Rick back into the living room.

Tayla thought Rick might have left with his nephew but he sat down on the lounge chair, relaxing back, crossing one long leg over the other. She tried not to look at him in case she gave her daughter any reason to suspect her involvement with this man.

'You know, you could have come to the movies with us,' Carey remarked amiably. 'What on earth did you do all night?'

Tayla's throat closed over completely and she valiantly willed herself not to blush.

'We talked.' Rick shrugged easily and Carey's gaze went from one to the other.

'Talked?' She grinned impishly. 'Now I'm getting very suspicious. Are you sure that's all you did?'

'Carey!' Tayla did blush then and Carey's grin widened.

'Mum, you're so easy to tease, do you know that?' She glanced at Rick. 'Sorry. It's a family joke. I should warn you Mum's sort of known as the puritan of the family.'

Tayla couldn't bring herself to look at Rick. And she was going to have very stern words with her daughter at the first opportunity.

'Thank you so much for sharing that with me,' Rick remarked dryly. 'But I don't think your mother is anything of the kind.'

To Tayla's amazement he turned and winked outrageously at her.

'I saw that!' Carey declared. 'What *have* you two been up to while I left you unchaperoned?' She looked at Rick with mock seriousness. 'Should I be asking you if your intentions are honourable?'

'Carey, I don't—' Tayla began as Rick grinned.

'Very honourable.'

'Hmm. I don't know if I believe that,' Carey said with a frown. 'It's a known fact men are only after one thing.'

'So cynical so young. And you know what else they say?' He raised his eyebrows at Carey. 'Abstinence makes the heart grow fonder.'

Carey blinked and then a huge grin lit her face. 'Wow! That was clever. You're not just a pretty face are you?'

'Definitely not,' he informed her with mock earnestness. 'I'm shy, sensitive, and in touch with my feelings.'

'Oh, no,' Carey groaned. 'Give me the brooding, silent type any day. Who wants to sit and listen to a guy talking about himself for hours on end.'

'Well, actually, that's never appealed to me, either.'

Carey looked across at him and opened her mouth to retaliate.

'I think we need a change of subject,' Tayla put in quickly. 'There's some lemonade left in the fridge if you'd like some, Carey.'

Carey grimaced. 'No, thanks, Mum.'

At that moment the telephone rang and Tayla glanced at the clock as she reached for the receiver. Who would be calling them this late at night? She thought of Nan and quelled a spurt of apprehension.

'Tayla Greer.'

'Oh, Tayla. It's Meg. Meg Lewis,' came the slightly breathless voice.

'Yes?' Tayla's gaze slid to Rick and away again.

'I'm sorry to ring you this late,' Meg continued. 'But I need to reach Rick. He's not at home and I know he was coming over to your place and I wondered if he was still there.'

'Yes. Yes, he is. Just a moment.' Tayla held the receiver out to Rick. 'It's for you. It's Meg.'

Rick stood up and took the phone, a slight frown on his face. 'Meg? What's wrong?'

Tayla didn't know whether to stay where she was or leave the room and give Rick some privacy. As she sat there she couldn't prevent herself from hearing Rick's side of the conversation. And Carey was openly listening with interest.

'When? Is he OK?' Rick chewed on his lower lip. 'I know. It's all right, Meg. I'll be right there.' He glanced at his wristwatch. 'About five or ten minutes.' He replaced the receiver and turned back to face Tayla.

'Tayla, I'm sorry. I have to go.'

CHAPTER ELEVEN

SHE took a shallow breath. 'Of course.'

'Young Aaron fell over and somehow broke his arm,' he explained. 'The doctors are about to set the break so Meg wants me to go and collect the other two kids and take them home. Meg's parents went out for the evening and she wants me to stay with the kids until their grandparents return.'

Tayla stood up and Rick moved towards the door, stopping to look back at her.

'I hope Meg's little boy will be all right,' Tayla got out and he ran his hand through his hair.

He looked as though he was about to say something else, and then he glanced quickly at Carey and sighed faintly. 'I'll ring you tomorrow.'

Tayla nodded and followed him to the door, closing it after him. She stood with her hand unconsciously resting on the doorknob. She felt surprisingly numb. How could she have forgotten Meg Lewis? Dear God! What had she done?

'Mum?' Carey's voice brought Tayla back to the present and she drew herself together before she turned to face her daughter.

'That's bad luck, isn't it? The little boy breaking his arm,' Tayla said lightly, suspecting she could very easily start to babble. She made herself walk back into the living room.

'Meg Lewis?' Carey frowned as she sat down again.

'That's Rick's secretary, isn't it? She was at the Christmas party, wasn't she?'

'That's right.'

'Oh.' Carey continued to frown. 'Isn't she the one whose husband was killed on a building site?'

'Yes. It must have been dreadful for her.' Tayla felt disembodied, as though she was standing outside herself carrying on the conversation.

'Ben told me about it. They were all friends, he said, at school and everything.'

'So Rick's grandmother told me.'

Carey shifted her position on the lounge chair, swinging her long legs over the arm. 'Is Rick going out with her?'

Tayla swallowed. 'I really don't know, love.'

Carey sighed loudly. 'Well, even if he did run off like that I don't think they are.' She looked across at her mother. 'Do you?'

Tayla shrugged, her heart sinking. 'As I said, I don't know.' Yet she suspected she did know. And a painful heaviness slowly enveloped her heart. With no little effort she smiled at her daughter. 'Well, tell me all about Ben.'

Carey coloured slightly. 'Ben's OK, Mum. He really is.'

Tayla expected to remain wide awake when she finally fell into bed, the same bed she'd shared short hours ago with Rick McCall. But she slipped almost immediately into a sound sleep.

All the unaccustomed exercise, she taunted herself when she woke up in the morning to the buzzing of cicadas and another hot summer day.

What time had Rick got home? she wondered. How

long had he had to stay with Meg Lewis's children? Did he have a relationship with the young widow? Meg's young family needed a father and Tayla had to admit Rick would be ideal. Had he gone home at all? Tayla tortured herself with her thoughts as she lie in bed trying to find the energy and inclination to get up.

Just before Carey arrived home Rick had said he wanted to see Tayla again. Had that been a spur of moment thing? The euphoric aftermath of great sex? Or would he come to his senses in the cold hard light of day?

Supposing he did want to see her, Tayla, again. Did she want to see him? Tayla moaned softly. Who was she kidding? Of course she did.

What a joke! And it was well and truly on her. She was in love with Rick McCall, a man nearly seven years younger than she was. How would they possibly—

She stopped herself finishing the thought. There was no possibility so she'd better get used to the idea, starting right now, before things went any further. Any further? She could almost laugh at that. How much further could they go than they had last night?

A tingle of awareness grew inside her as she remembered the way he'd made her feel. She'd told him the truth. She'd never felt that way before. Mike was the only man she'd ever made love with and he'd never evoked such a response, such passion.

She shivered and determinedly climbed out of bed. And she just as determinedly decided to put all thoughts of Rick McCall out of her mind. She would throw herself into Christmas preparations. Christmas Day was fast approaching and soon Nan would be arriving down to stay. There was much to be done.

'But do I absolutely have to come?' Carey asked as Tayla picked up her car keys.

'You know Nan's coming to stay with us this year so we need provisions for Christmas. And—' Tayla grimaced at her daughter '—we need to make some traditional Christmas fare.'

'Traditional fare? You mean you want me to cook?' Carey looked horrified. 'You know I can't cook for nuts, Mum.'

'I need you to *help* me cook,' Tayla explained. 'Look upon it as furthering your education in the journey of life.'

Carey groaned. 'The journey of life? The trip from hell, you mean, don't you? Mum, this is child abuse.'

'Child abuse would be if you had no Christmas dinner at all.' Tayla laughed. 'Come on. Hop in the car. I promise you, you'll love it.'

When they returned Tayla casually checked the answering machine. One hang up. No message from Rick.

After lunch Carey set off to put in the afternoon at the print shop where she worked part-time. Tayla sat down at the kitchen table and began to make a list of what she had to do for Christmas and in what order it had to be done. Compiling a list should motivate her into making a start.

Yet she kept remembering and her body responded accordingly. Was this simply the normal reactions of someone who'd been on their own for five years?

Tayla thought she'd loved her late husband. And she had, she told herself. Or perhaps she'd just been youthfully in love with the idea of being in love.

Mike had loved her. She knew that. But he hadn't been as, well, as interested in sex. It had only been a small part of his life.

This thing between herself and Rick was— She paused. *Once in a lifetime.* The thought slipped into her mind and she couldn't seem to dislodge it. She suspected her feelings for Rick *were* once in a lifetime. That thought scared her. And the idea that he might feel the same way terrified her even more.

A truck pulled into the street and drove slowly past, stopping a few houses down. And suddenly there came the sound of a well-known Christmas carol. Each year the Salvation Army Band travelled throughout the suburbs playing carols, band members clustered on the back of a truck, another Christmas tradition.

Absently Tayla walked over to her wallet to get a donation for the door-knock appeal. She stood and looked down at the money in her hand and then she was crying, tears rolling down her face as the joyous strains of *God Rest Ye Merry Gentlemen* skipped across the heatwaves that were synonymous with Australia's Christmastime.

Yet she couldn't have defined specifically what it was that made her feel so sorrowful. Perhaps the realisation of the depth of her feelings for Rick made her acknowledge that she had made a last farewell to Mike. Or maybe it was the fact that she couldn't see a future for herself with the one man she suspected could mean something to her, might give her the kind of love she now realised she had always coveted.

Eventually she pulled herself together and she quickly splashed her face with tepid water before going to the door and smiling a Merry Christmas at the young woman who was collecting for the appeal. With a sigh she went back into the kitchen and tried to concentrate on her list.

She was simply being fanciful, she told herself firmly. She just needed to get this whole thing with Rick McCall into a realistic sense of proportion, she admonished herself yet again. He was an attractive man. She was a lonely widow. That was the sum of it. And as for everlasting love, well, that was the fantasy.

Resolutely she stood up again and collected the ingredients for their favourite Christmas confectionery, *White Christmas*. She began to measure out the copha, the mixed fruit, and she was slipping the baking trays into the refrigerator when the phone rang.

The kitchen clock told her it was after three and she stared at the phone for long moments before wiping her fingers on a handtowel and picking up the extension.

'Tayla. It's Rick.' His deep voice drove whatever perspective she'd attained right out the window and she sank down onto the nearest kitchen chair.

'Oh. Hello,' she said flatly and grimaced at herself. 'How's Meg's little boy?'

'He's OK. She's taking him home this afternoon.' He paused. 'Tayla, about last night. I'm sorry I had to— Look, when can we see each other again? Will you have dinner with me tonight?'

'Rick, I— I've been thinking about that and I, well, I don't think it's a good idea.'

There was a moment's silence. 'Why not?' he asked quietly.

'It's just too complicated. I— There's too much involved. Carey. Our ages.'

'I see.' A long silence echoed in her ear and then she heard him sigh. 'Tayla—'

Someone spoke in the background and he covered the receiver. Tayla heard muffled voices, followed by a door closing, and then he came back on the line.

'Something's come up and I have to go. But Tayla, I'm not going to give up that easily. I'll see you soon.'

Tayla sat there looking at the buzzing telephone as a mass of conflicting emotions catapulted about inside her. And yet the only thought that stayed with her was the one that she loved him and wanted desperately to be with him.

Would it be so terrible? she asked herself. Lots of other women married younger men. Married? Tayla forced herself to her feet and angrily began to clear away her cooking ingredients. She was acting like an adolescent. She barely knew the man and now she was hearing wedding bells.

She'd just finished dressing after having a quick shower when the doorbell rang. Tayla walked out to see Rick standing on the veranda. He'd discarded his tie and his white shirt was open at the throat, the sleeves rolled up over his elbows.

Tayla glanced at the time. What was he doing here? Surely he should be at work?

'I've absconded. Left early,' he said with a crooked smile, apparently reading her mind. 'I had to see you.'

Reluctantly Tayla opened the door. 'Rick, you shouldn't have come.'

'Maybe not. But I had to. Is Carey home?'

Tayla shook her head. 'She's at work.'

He nodded. 'Can we go inside?'

After a moment Tayla stood back, closing the screen door after him, following him into the living room.

He stood with his back to her, his hands shoved into the pockets of his slacks.

'Now, tell me why you think it's not such a good idea for us to see each other again,' he said levelly, as he slowly turned to face her.

'You know as well as I do,' Tayla began. 'It just won't work.'

'It seemed to be working rather well last night, I would have thought,' he said dryly.

'I'll admit last night was—' Tayla drew a steadying breath. 'It was really nice and—'

'Nice?' He cut in on her. 'Last night was incredible.'

'Rick, you can't just build a relationship on good sex. There are other things to be taken into consideration.'

'Like what?'

'I've got a teenage daughter. I'm seven years older than you. Lots of things,' Tayla finished in a rush.

'I think your teenage daughter is great. And I don't think she dislikes me. With regard to the age thing, it's a fact women live longer than men do, so I'd say we're fairly evenly matched in that respect.'

'Rick, please—'

'I love you, Tayla.'

Tayla's heart lurched in her breast. If only she could believe he meant that. 'You only think you do,' she said, her voice a little thin in her ears.

'This is an observation from the knowledge of your advanced years,' he remarked mockingly and Tayla ran a hand agitatedly through her hair.

'No. It's simply common sense. I'm unattainable so—'

'Unattainable?' Rick bit off an oath. 'Tayla, I'm not a pimply adolescent who's all hot and bothered over his first roll in the hay.'

'I didn't say—'

'I love you, Tayla. I've never said that to another woman,' he said earnestly. 'I've thought about saying it a couple of times but I've never said it. I've loved other women but not the way I love you. Nothing like this, this need to be with you, to hear you laugh, to watch the way your eyes crinkle at the corners, to want to feel that gorgeous body of yours next to mine. I want to love you, cherish you, grow old with you.'

'I'll be old before you,' Tayla put in quickly.

'Not the way things are going. I'll be on my last legs way before my time. I've aged years in the short time since I met you.'

'And that's another point. We barely know each other.'

He raised his hands in exasperation and let them fall. 'I know I've never felt this way about anyone before. And I do know you. I know you have that little freckle right—'

'Rick!' Tayla held up her hand and he looked at her. She swallowed again. 'What will people say?'

'Who gives a stuff what people say? What people anyway?'

'Our families. Friends.'

'It's not our problem. And besides, I'd say they'd just be happy for us.'

How Tayla wanted to believe him.

'Your— Someone said you were, well— You were involved with Meg Lewis,' Tayla said breathily.

His gaze held hers levelly and then he sighed. 'That's a fair enough question,' he conceded. 'Maybe we should sit down.'

Rick chose the couch when Tayla took the single chair opposite him.

'Meg and I have been friends for a long time,' he began. 'Her husband, Trevor, was my best friend. Trev's family lived next door to our place and we were good mates before we even started school.

'When we were about nine or ten Meg's family arrived from the U.K. and bought a house in our street. Our families became friends with Meg's family.'

He smiled faintly. 'Meg could climb trees faster than we could and she rode her bicycle like a professional. Trev and I were impressed so she became a mate, too. Her mother used to call us the Three Musketeers.

'Then we got to be about thirteen or fourteen.' He grimaced. 'A very susceptible age for Trev and me. We both decided Meg was going to be our girlfriend so we started vying for her favours. But Meg was way ahead of us by then and she took a fancy to an older guy who played on the school football team.'

He shook his head. 'Trevor and I were a bit put out about that and we made a pact to swear off fickle females for the rest of our lives.

'Then the three of us went our separate ways for a while. Meg went overseas to visit relatives in London, Trevor started work as an apprentice electrician and I went to university. But Trev and I kept in touch.

'Meg returned home to Australia in time for Trev's twenty-first birthday. We hadn't seen her for a couple of years and we both decided again that she would be our girlfriend.

'A year later Trevor asked Meg to marry him and she accepted. I thought my heart was broken but it healed pretty quickly so—' He shrugged. 'Everyone said the usual things about Meg and Trev getting married. They were too young, et cetera, et cetera, but they were the perfect match.

'Back then I used to tease Trev about being tied down with a wife and family. But he'd just laugh and slap me on the back and tell me to wait until cupid's arrow got me and then I'd know how great it was. Part of me used to envy Meg's and Trevor's closeness. They loved each other and adored their kids. Trevor was over the moon when Shaynah was born.'

He looked across at Tayla but she suspected he wasn't consciously seeing her. 'Trev was working on a project on the other side of the city and I was over that way so I called in to see him. He was showing me over the site, pointing out how they'd incorporated the old building with the new additions, telling me how they'd kept as many of the trees and shrubs as they could.

'It was a windy day and a bough fell from an old gum tree.' He shook his head slightly. 'The widow-maker they call those branches. Very apt. I was standing beside Trevor and we both heard the noise, the timber cracking. One minute we were standing talking and the next we were both on the ground. All I got was a scratch or two but Trev never regained consciousness.'

'Oh, Rick.' Tayla stood up, sat next to him on the couch and put her hand on his shoulder. 'I'm sorry.'

He nodded. 'Trevor was a great bloke. I wish you could have met him. And I wish he could have known you.'

Rick took a deep breath. 'I had to go and tell Meg what had happened. That was the hardest thing I've ever done in my life. As you can imagine she was devastated but she's been great, kept going, tried to keep everything as normal as possible for the kids.

'I felt guilty for ages afterwards, that Trev, who had everything to live for, had been killed and I was alive. I guess I overcompensated by trying to do and be every-thing for Meg.' He looked down at his hands clasped between his knees. 'Everyone then started surmising about the possibility of Meg and I getting together.

'That sort of shook me. I knew I wasn't in love with Meg, not the way Trevor loved her, and I realised I had to get away, think things through, be sure about what I wanted to do before I spoke to Meg. That's why I went up north on that holiday. It gave me breathing space, time to think, and when I came back I had a long talk to Meg. We decided marrying would only spoil our long-standing friendship.'

He turned back to face Tayla. 'When I met you I knew what Trev was talking about,' he said simply. 'Cupid struck a bullseye.'

Tayla felt tears well up behind her eyes. 'Rick, I—' She shook her head. 'I don't think it would be sensible for us to get involved. As I said before, you're, well, young and—'

'And willing.'

'Willing? What—' Tayla swallowed. 'What do you mean?'

'I mean willing. Like Dickens's Barkis.'

Their eyes met.

'Marry me, Tayla.'

CHAPTER TWELVE

'MARRY you? Rick, are you mad?' She stood up, her legs suddenly shaky, and took a few paces across the carpet, away from him.

'Mad with wanting you.'

She turned back to face him. 'You can't be serious.'

'I've never been more serious in my life.' He walked across and took her hand in his, lifted it to his lips, kissed it tenderly. 'I knew the first time I saw you that you were the one woman I'd been waiting for all my life. And as I got to know you, saw you with Carey, with your family, I knew for sure I wanted to be part of your life. Of course, the cake capped it off.'

Tayla blinked. 'What cake?'

'Remember our midnight snack up at Nan's? You gave me some of the cake you'd made.' He grinned crookedly. 'One mouthful of that cake and I had to have you.'

Tayla laughed despite herself. 'I feel I should warn you that I only cook on special occasions.'

'Then I'm going to be sure I'm there whenever the occasions are special,' he said softly as he gazed down at her and Tayla felt her heart jolt in her chest.

'Apart from that,' he continued, 'I want to spend the rest of my life with you and Carey. I know Carey doesn't need a father. I wouldn't even begin to try to fill that role. And I wouldn't try to replace him.'

'Rick—'

'Please, Tayla. Let me finish. I know Carey had a

father, a very good one if the way she's turned out is anything to go by. Although I'd say her wonderful mother had a lot to do with that. And I know you had a good husband,' he said softly and a wave of pain passed over Tayla's face.

He seemed to flinch and a frown furrowed his brow. 'I know you loved him, Tayla, but your husband isn't here now. And I am. Surely he wouldn't want you to throw yourself on his funeral pyre.' He stepped closer to her, almost touching her. But not quite.

And Tayla wanted him to. So much. Yet she couldn't allow it. She shook her head as a riot of emotions churned about inside her.

'Mike was a good husband,' she said carefully. 'He— But he was a quiet, serious person. He worked very hard, long hours, so—' She looked up at him. 'But he was a good man.'

A pulse throbbed in his jaw. 'Did your good husband have this very same effect on you?' he asked intensely, his voice low, his eyes relentlessly holding her gaze.

'What— I don't know what you mean.'

'Yes, you do, Tayla.' He ran one fingertip lightly down her bare arm from shoulder to wrist, settled on the pulse that beat there. 'Did he set you on fire the way I do?'

'Don't do this to me, Rick.'

He lowered his head, his teeth gently teasing her sensitive earlobe. 'Do what?'

'What you're doing.'

His mouth slowly, agonisingly slowly, followed the curve of her cheek. 'Do you honestly want me to stop?'

'Yes. No.' Tayla groaned. 'I don't know. No, don't. Don't stop.'

His arms came around her, his lips finally finding hers

and they clung together. Tayla's entire body was on fire and she was exhilarated and yet terrified by the depth of passion he aroused within her. At that moment she could no more have stopped him kissing her than she could have caught the moon.

Rick sank down on the couch again, drawing her down beside him, his lips nuzzling the curve of her neck.

'Dear God! You feel so good,' he murmured thickly and his voice only served to fan the flame of her desire.

'Rick.' Tayla's fingers twined in his soft, thick hair, and she breathed in the musky male scent of him. 'What you do to me. I can't seem to—'

'Then marry me, Tayla. I love you and nothing less will do.'

He looked up at her, his eyes aglow and the depth of feeling Tayla saw reflected there suddenly seemed to disperse any doubts she'd had. It was as though she was alleviated from the cheerlessness, the sombreness of the past. A heavy shadow lifted from her, setting her free, leaving her light and filled with a wondrous sense of great happiness.

'I love you, too, Rick,' she said brokenly.

He closed his eyes for one long moment and then kissed her lingeringly.

'Do you—' She swallowed. 'Will it work, Rick?'

'Like clockwork.' He grinned broadly. 'You have my promise.'

She laughed uncertainly.

'May I take that as a yes then?' He raised his dark eyebrows and she nodded.

'I think you might.'

He kissed her again and it was some time before they were capable of further speech.

'So when did you fall for me?' he asked, his expression one of mock cockiness and Tayla made a show of giving the question very serious thought.

'Well, now. Let's see if I can remember.'

He gave a disbelieving laugh. 'It was love at first sight. I could tell.'

She ran her fingertip along the curve of his jaw. 'Is there no end to your talents? Not only handsome but smart as all get-out,' she teased and then sobered. 'It was when you took off that motorcycle helmet and turned to look up at me with those beautiful blue eyes of yours, and you smiled your incredible smile.'

Rick flushed a little and a smile played around his mouth. 'And there I was all long-haired and unshaven.' He looked into her eyes. 'And feeling as though I'd been hit in the solar plexus. I wanted to lift you in my arms, deposit you on the back of the bike, and ride away with you into the sunset.'

'I have a feeling in those first few moments I would even have gone with you, sunset or not,' Tayla said softly and placed a tender kiss on the edge of his chin.

'Mmm.' He drew her impossibly closer. 'Now that we have all that settled, my next question is, how soon are you going to make an honest man of me?'

'An honest man of *you?*' Tayla repeated, her breath escaping on a gasp of disbelief. 'I'd say I was the fallen person in this equation. I seem to remember you were the cad who had his evil,' she paused and gave him a slow smile, 'but so very divine, way with me.'

'It'll never stand up in court. You were older so you should have known better,' he remarked piously and Tayla spluttered.

Rick gave a throaty laugh and Tayla leaned closer, letting her lips linger on his in a slow kiss.

'As it happens,' she said softly, 'I think I did know better, don't you? Did I lead you very far astray? Hmm?'

Rick's eyes darkened. 'Well and truly off the track. But do you know something, my darling Tayla, I'm not even going to try to find my way back.'

They kissed each other again and Tayla felt as though she sank into him, that they merged with each other.

With a slight grimace Rick shifted on the couch, settling them more comfortably. 'I don't suppose there's any chance you might lead me astray again any time soon, is there?' he asked and Tayla pretended virtuous outrage.

'Now?' she asked in mock horror.

Rick glanced around. 'We're alone. Carey's at work. Tell me you're not expecting an influx of visitors?'

'Well,' she considered slowly. 'If we're in the back of the house, say in my bedroom, we wouldn't have to answer the doorbell, would we?'

'Ah. The old selective hearing technique.' He stood up and pulled her to her feet and back into his arms. 'And since I've created the precedent, do I have to carry you along the hallway like I did last time?'

Tayla's lips lifted in a mischievous grin. 'Oh, let's conserve your strength for other things.'

'I see. You have another job for me. You want me to move another cupboard?'

Tayla shook her head and kissed him lightly on the earlobe. 'I did have in mind you moving something but not the cupboard exactly.'

'No?' He grinned down at her. 'My mind boggles.'

'How about moving the earth for me again, hmm?' Tayla asked him huskily.

'The earth? My forte,' he said nonchalantly and grinned as they walked out into the hallway, his strong arm wrapped around her. 'Yes,' he stated enthusiastically. 'I have a feeling I'm going to enjoy this job.'

EPILOGUE

CAREY knocked softly on the bedroom door and Tayla called to her daughter to come in. The young girl walked over to the bassinette and murmured to the baby, smiling as he wrapped his tiny fingers around one of hers.

'Ben's coming over and he won't be here for about an hour so would you like me to give Jake his bottle?'

She glanced up to see her mother grinning at her and she frowned.

'What?' she asked inquiringly.

'Ben's coming over again?' Tayla said lightly. 'You're seeing a lot of him these days, aren't you?'

'We're working on a computer program for his father,' Carey said quickly.

'Carey, about—' Tayla began and Carey shrugged.

'Ben and I are just good friends, Mum. Quit worrying about me. I'm a big girl now.'

'A mother's prerogative. And I'm not really worried. Just...' Tayla paused. 'Interested.'

'Oh. Right, Mum.' Carey grinned roguishly at her mother. 'If we decide to elope you'll be the first to know.'

'An elopement. Well, that will save me the cost of the wedding,' Tayla answered in kind. 'Seriously, love. I do like Ben.'

'I know.' Carey flushed a little and then smiled sheepishly. 'Actually, he's pretty nice, for a guy.'

'Who? Jake's father?' teased Rick as he came into the room and Carey gave him a shove.

185

'No. Jake's father's nephew, if you must know,' she replied. 'And unfortunately, it doesn't run in the family.'

'Oh, I'm wounded.' Rick put his hand on his heart. 'But did I hear you say Ben's okay for a guy? Wow! This sounds serious. Perhaps I'd better have a little chat with young Ben, man to man.'

Carey looked up at him momentarily horrified and then she laughed reluctantly. 'One to you, Rick. You almost had me there.' She looked at him levelly. 'You wouldn't, would you?'

'No.' He laughed. 'But I can have a chat with his father.'

'Don't you dare. Or else I'll…well—' Carey pursed her lips and then chuckled. 'Or I won't baby-sit Jake for you.'

'Ah. Blackmail. What a low blow.'

The baby made a little chortling sound as Carey bent over him again. 'Do you think he recognised his daddy in the red suit and curly white whiskers last night?'

'I'm sure he did.' Tayla grinned and tenderly cupped Rick's cheek with her hand. 'But he wasn't telling.'

'Smart kid.' Rick moved his head and placed a soft kiss in the palm of Tayla's hand.

'Did you notice the number of babies at the Christmas party last night?' Carey was saying. 'You know, I can't understand why people keep having these little rug-rats. They're so labour-intensive and time-consuming.'

Tayla chuckled. 'They are that,' she agreed.

Carey carefully lifted the baby out of his bassinette. She snuggled him into her and breathed in his clean baby scent. 'But I have to admit, this one of ours is very cute,' she acknowledged.

'Just like his daddy,' said Tayla with a smirk and Rick's brows drew together in mock deliberation.

'So you really think I'm cute, Mrs. McCall?'

'Very cute,' she said softly and reached up to kiss him.

'Mmm.' Rick put his arms around her and pulled her into his body.

They looked into each other's eyes and Tayla's heartbeats flipped over themselves. This past year with Rick had been incredible and she'd been happier than she could ever have imagined she'd be.

'Oh! Oh! The two lovebirds are at it again. Come on, little brother. Let's go get your bottle.' Carey headed for the door. Grinning teasingly she stopped to look back at Rick and her mother. 'And if those two keep looking at each other like that, Jake, we're going to have a whole tribe of little McCalls, just like you.'

Harlequin® Historical

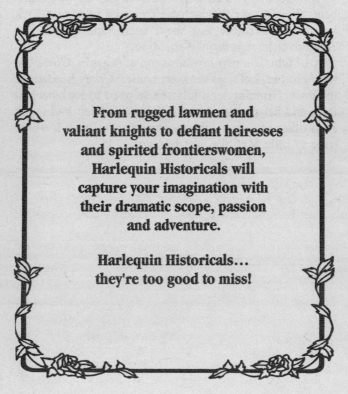

From rugged lawmen and
valiant knights to defiant heiresses
and spirited frontierswomen,
Harlequin Historicals will
capture your imagination with
their dramatic scope, passion
and adventure.

Harlequin Historicals…
they're too good to miss!

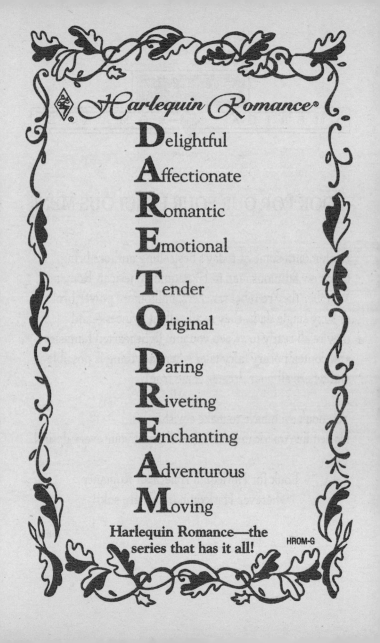

Harlequin Romance®

Delightful

Affectionate

Romantic

Emotional

Tender

Original

Daring

Riveting

Enchanting

Adventurous

Moving

Harlequin Romance—the
series that has it all!

HROM-G

HARLEQUIN®

A M E R I C A N ◆ R O M A N C E®

LOOK FOR OUR FOUR FABULOUS MEN!

Each month some of today's bestselling authors bring four new fabulous men to Harlequin American Romance. Whether they're rebel ranchers, millionaire power brokers or sexy single dads, they're all gallant princes—and they're all ready to sweep you into lighthearted fantasies and contemporary fairy tales where anything is possible and where all your dreams come true!

You don't even have to make a wish…
Harlequin American Romance will grant your every desire!

Look for Harlequin American Romance
wherever Harlequin books are sold!

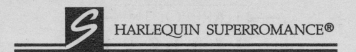
HARLEQUIN SUPERROMANCE®

...there's more to the story!

Superromance. A *big* satisfying read about unforgettable characters. Each month we offer *four* very different stories that range from family drama to adventure and mystery, from highly emotional stories to romantic comedies—and much more! Stories about people you'll believe in and care about. Stories too compelling to put down....

Our authors are among today's *best* romance writers. You'll find familiar names and talented newcomers. Many of them are award winners—and you'll see why!

If you want the biggest and best in romance fiction, you'll get it from Superromance!

Available wherever Harlequin books are sold.